THE OTHERWORLDLY HOUSEHOLD

A No-nonsense Guide to Enchanting the Witch's Home

KITTY FIELDS
FOR OTHERWORLDLY ORACLE
Copyright 2023

Contents

Chapter 1 2
What is the Otherworldly Household? 2
   The Structure of a Home 3
Chapter 2 6
Protection 6
   Cleansing 6
      How to Perform a House Cleansing 7
      Other Home Cleansing Methods 8
   Warding and Sealing... 12
      How to Perform a Warding of Your Property and Home 13
      Sealing 16
      Home Protection Powder Recipe & A Sealing Ritual 18
   Protective Charms.. 19
      The Traditional Witch Bottle 22
      How to Make Your Own Witch Bottle 23
   Inviting Protective Spirits and Guardians 24
Chapter 3 29
Household Spirits 29
   Household Gods and Goddesses 29
   Household Faeries and Elves 31
   How a House Acquires Its Spirits 37
      Ancestors at the Hearth 37
      Your House's Spirit 38
   Feeding Your Household Spirits 39

Room for House Faeries	39
Chapter 4	40
Magical Themes and Colors	40
Magical Décor Themes	40
Color Magic in the Home	42
Chapter 5	50
The Otherworldly Kitchen	50
Quick, Cheap Ways to Shift the Vibe in Your Kitchen	50
Organization, Purification and Cleanliness	51
Kitchen Altars	52
Space for Household Spirits and Fae	52
Kitchen Appliance Magic	53
The Fridge and Freezer	53
Stove and Oven	56
Sink and Dishwasher	57
A Kitchen Witch's Tools	57
Kitchen Witch Guardian Dolls	65
More Kitchen Witch Tools and Ingredients	67
Chapter 6	68
The Living Room	68
The Ancestral Altar	69
Charms for Peace and Harmony	71
Chapter 7	74
The Bathroom	74
Bathroom Decorations	75
Water Gods and Goddesses	77

The Tub and Shower 79

The Toilet 80

The Bathroom Mirror 81

Chapter 8 83

The Bedroom 83

Magical Bedroom Decorations 84

The Bed 85

The Dresser Drawers 86

The Closet and Wardrobe 87

Chapter 9 89

The "Other" Rooms 89

Chapter 10 91

The Garden 91

Attracting Fae to the Otherworldly Garden 92

Faery Food and Libations: 93

What NOT To Do When Attracting the Faeries 94

Wrapping It Up 96

Chapter 1

What is the Otherworldly Household?

We spend most of our lives in our homes. It's the comfy, cozy place where we sleep, eat, rest, recover when we are ill, and simply spend our time. We bond with family, make memories, and share love in our homes. We are protected from the outside world, from harsh weather and intruders, within the walls of our homes. We know when we close and lock the door, we are safe and sound. So why not treat your home as though it's a living, breathing being…perhaps even a friend? Or a family member? Why not acknowledge and harness the true magic within its walls?

In this book, my goal is to give you my personal recommendations on how to enchant your home and make it into an Otherworldly place. Please keep in mind, I'm not telling you to go out and spend all your money on new witchcraft tools or decorations. Take what you will from this book and apply it to your own home, in your own way. And leave the rest.

What is an Otherworldly Household, exactly? It's a home where the witch feels safe and secure, but also a place where the witch communes easily with the Otherworld. It's a home that's somewhere between here and there. A liminal place but also a protected, sacred space.

Do you remember a particularly special home from your childhood? One where you felt you could be yourself – thoroughly protected, able to play, learn and love? For me, my grandmother's house comes to mind. Her home was filled with love and magic. I recall many days and nights of playing in the garden, hiding under large pine trees, collecting dogwood flowers, and plucking juicy, scarlet tomatoes right off the vine. Standing under giant sunflowers that towered over me. Peering out my second-floor bedroom window, dreaming I was Rapunzel locked up in my tower. It was a place I could sleep soundly and dream of wild things. A home where I could let my imagination roam free. And there were spirits there. Oh, the spirits there were some of the first I ever met on my witchcraft journey.

When you think of a magical home, what comes to mind? The Sanderson Sisters' rustic colonial cottage in Hocus Pocus? A sprawling, dark Victorian home with a wraparound porch? A small cabin with a fireplace? Let your idea or image of the perfect magical home inspire you. Then manifest it and turn your home into an Otherworldly Household.

The Structure of a Home

Let's talk about the structure of a house. A house consists of a roof, walls, floors, windows, and doors. When we enter a house, we see more walls, doors and the like that creates rooms within. Each structural component of the Otherworldly Household serves an important purpose, physically and spiritually.

We'll start with the roof. The roof prevents rain, snow, and sleet from falling in. It keeps the sun from beating down on us, and in general, keeps our homes free of dirt and debris. These are its physical features. The roof is a barrier between us and the sky. Just on the other side of the roof lies the ether. And beyond that, the clouds, wind, sun, stars, and moon on a clear night. Just beyond the roof is the entire Universe.

In my opinion, the walls are probably the most important part of the house's structure. If you didn't have walls, you wouldn't have a whole home. Walls block out weather, wildlife, and intruders. Walls give us a space to feel safe and warm. Sort of like our own burrow or den. Some folks have four walls, others have more or less, depending on the layout and size of the home. Magically, witches have hidden magical charms and spells in walls for centuries.

The floor is the last major structural component of the house. In centuries past, the floor was the earth itself – dirt, grass, stone, or dust. Today, we stand on manufactured floors constructed of concrete and wood, topped with tile, hardwood, or carpeting. It keeps our feet clean and comfortable. Spiritually, the floor is a barrier between us and the earth. While a barrier between us and Mother Earth might seem like a bad thing, it's not. Sit on the floor of your home and feel your roots growing down through the floor and into the earth below. The effect is nearly as strong as grounding yourself outside on the bare earth. In addition, the floor magically protects us from chthonic spirits when you've charged it with this intention.

Have you ever heard people say the eyes are the window to the soul? Well, for the Otherworldly Household, the windows are the house's eyes that allow us to see its soul (its residents inside). Have you ever passed an old house and felt the windows were its eyes, watching you? When we are inside, the windows allow us to look out and see the world. Windows let the sunshine in and a cool breeze on a hot summer's day. Modern windows are typically made of glass, an amazing substance made from melted sand, soil, and stone. Glass is connected to the earth element but also to water because of its sand content and the melting process.

Now you understand the structure of the Otherworldly Household. But also think about the materials that went into the construction of your home. There is a combination of different kinds of wood, metal, glass, plastic, and stone. What's in your house's walls, floors, roof, etc.? Remember, the natural materials that went into the construction of your home came from the earth. The wood from trees. The glass from sand. The metal from the earth's crust. Which means, these materials once housed a land spirit or an elemental. Sometimes an elemental's energy clings onto the wood or stone harvested by man's hands and is then transferred into your house during construction. Many unique energies make up the spiritual ecosystem of the Otherworldly Household. And each spirit should be acknowledged and honored.

Chapter 2

Potent Household Protection

Your home protects you and cares for you twenty-four-seven, but do you reciprocate? Regular maintenance and repairs are required to keep your home in top condition. A structure that's been neglected or in disrepair will only protect you for a short time. Therefore, your first responsibility is to care for the physicality of your home. Keep it clean, organized, decluttered, and keep up on your repairs as best you can. If you care for your home, it will care for you.

In this chapter, we will learn how to spiritually protect your home and property. This section will be broken down into four parts: cleansing, warding, sealing and invocation. Each component of your home protection ritual is crucial. The more time and effort you put into protecting your home, the stronger your physical and spiritual walls will be. You'll also find your own way of doing things. How I cleanse, ward and seal my home might be completely different from how you do it. And that's okay. We don't have practice the same brand of witchcraft for our magic to be effective.

Cleansing

Just as homes need to be physically cleaned, they also need to be spiritually cleaned. We call this *cleansing*. Performing a house cleansing will remove negative energy and any uninvited spirits that might be lurking in your sacred space. Let's learn how to perform a house cleansing, house blessing, and how to spiritually protect your home from invasion.

Negative energy may build up in a home where trauma occurred, including domestic abuse, substance abuse and addiction, suicide or homicide, unexpected death and/or debilitating, long-term illness. A house cleansing will remove much of this negative energy. And, while a house blessing will bring in positive energy, active spiritual protection prevents further intrusion. What you need to know? Cleansing, blessing, and protection magic = a happy, Otherworldly Household = a happy, empowered you!

In addition to performing a house cleansing and blessing when moving into a new home, it should also be done when a new person moves in. New people will bring new energy into your home, and until the energy they bring stabilizes, it's a good idea to do a house cleansing. If there's a tragedy in the house, perform a house cleansing. If you're experiencing paranormal activity, try a house cleansing. I even recommend performing a routine house cleansing once a month on the waning or new moon, as well. But basically, any time you feel the energy in the home is heavy or chaotic, a house cleansing will re-set the atmosphere of your home. I think you get the point.

How to Perform a House Cleansing

A personal favorite of mine is to perform a good ol' fashioned smoke-cleansing ritual. Smoke-cleansing is a tradition of lighting herb bundles and allowing the smoke to purify a space. Different herbs are used for smoke-cleansings, including cedar, rosemary, lavender, rose, sage, sweetgrass, palo santo and juniper. If you can't get your hands on a dried herb bundle, make your own. The idea is to let the aromatic smoke fill each room with its purifying power. Incense can be used in place of an herb bundle, though I find the amount of smoke produced by an herb bundle is quicker and more effective for large spaces.

Follow these steps:

1. Open a few windows in your house and/or the back door. DON'T SKIP THIS STEP. It allows the negative energy to escape. It doesn't just dissipate. It has to go somewhere. Also, consider removing your smoke alarm for this process, if indeed you have a sensitive smoke alarm. It will likely go off. DON'T FORGET TO REPLACE IT when you're done! Safety first.
2. Start at your front door with your smoking bundle in-hand. Allow the smoke to fill the room and say, "I cleanse this home with smoke. All negativity must go away, only positive energy can stay." (Pro tip: I've found trying to light an herb bundle with a lighter doesn't keep the bundle smoking for long. Instead, light your herb bundle with the flame of a candle.)
3. Move in a counterclockwise direction from room to room. Allow the smoke to fill the air in each room while repeating the cleansing prayer above. Take the herb bundle in one hand and move it in a circular motion counterclockwise while speaking the words.
4. Don't forget the corners of each room, as well as the closets, cabinets, pantries, shower stalls, etc. This step is extra important if you're experiencing issues with unwanted spirits.
5. Once you've cleansed each room with smoke, extinguish the herb bundle and say, "so mote it be" or "amen" or "and it will be done". Whatever you feel most comfortable with.

Other Home Cleansing Methods

There are dozens of ways to successfully cleanse your home of negative energy. And plenty that don't involve burning herbs or smoke. If smoke is bothersome to you or a family member, try one of the following cleansing methods instead.

Make a simmering potpourri. This is also called a simmer pot or witch's pot. Heat a pot of water over the stove and bring it to a simmer. Then add aromatic herbs, fruit slices, salts, and any other protective ingredients to the pot. Allow the steam to fill your kitchen and home with its protective, aromatic vibrations. When done, let the remnants cool. I like to strain out the herbs and pour the liquid into a spray bottle, then spritz each room of my house. This concoction will keep in your fridge for at least three days if you'd like to continue using it over the week.

Some of my favorite ingredients for simmer pots include rosemary sprigs, bay leaves, pink salt, lemon and orange slices, cloves, apple slices and cinnamon sticks. But you should experiment with your own herbs and spell ingredients. Also consider using different kinds of magical waters. You might try simmering your herbs in moon water, sun water, or water collected from magical places like the ocean, a creek or river. Don't forget to take notes in your grimoire on the exact ingredients used and the results achieved so you can repeat or tweak it later.

The quickest way to cleanse your home of negative vibrations is by using *sound*. Have you ever been in a terrible mood and suddenly your favorite song comes on the radio? And your mood immediately shifts? That is the power of the vibration produced by sound. If the vibe in your Otherworldly Household feels heavy or in discord, play some high vibrational music to lift spirits and refresh the positive. Try different kinds of music including Norse pagan music, Celtic flutes, Shamanic drumming, meditation music, singing bowls, and nature sounds.

It's not just these beautiful melodies that have a cleansing effect on the home. Loud, obnoxious sounds have a purifying effect too, believe it or not. An old tradition of scaring off ghosts calls for the individual to bang on pots and pans. Or slam the doors unexpectedly. Though, conversely, some folks claim the ghosts in their homes aren't scared of banging doors, because the ghosts themselves slam them in the middle of the night. The same goes with pots and pans. If you have a ghost that enjoys making a raucous, it likely won't be scared off by the same noise it makes tormenting the living. However, I've used the pots-and-pans method to success with negative energy and lost, wandering spirits. Give it a try.

In addition to loud noises and high-vibing music, ringing bells has a cleansing effect in any space. Not to mention, bells are easy to use and portable. In European folklore, the sound of a bell was said to frighten the faery folk. This idea likely comes from the Early Modern Era belief that faeries were scared of the Christian God. And therefore, whenever they heard a ringing bell, they associated the sound with church bells and with the Christian God.

Witches ring bells to clear a space of negative energy, alert others that a ritual is beginning, and to sometimes to initiate a ritual or spell. Bells are made of metal, glass, and other materials. Choose your bell wisely. You may also want to consider wind chimes at the front and back doors. Chimes raise the vibration and ward off negative energy before it has a chance to enter the home. I find the high-pitched chimes allow for elemental energy to flow freely through your house, while the low-pitched chimes ward off nearly *all* spirits, elemental or otherwise. If you want the faeries to enter your home when invoked, opt for the higher pitched, twinkly chimes.

Sometimes a white candle and your intention is enough. Once, I was away from home and I was being tormented by a spirit. I was under psychic attack. I was experiencing the worst bout of sleep paralysis, nightmares, and night terrors I'd ever had in my life. I was scared to go to sleep…something that hadn't happened since I was a little girl. And I didn't have my herb bundles, bells, and other cleansing tools on-hand. The next best thing I could do was light a white candle and go from room to room, lighting up each space with divine white light energy. Along with the candlelight, I prayed to my gods and guides until I felt peaceful and empowered. That night I was freed from the nightmares and psychic attack.

Store bought herbal sprays work wonders too. Though, in my experience, the herbal sprays alone do not prevent from spirit attachment when traveling to haunted places. They do, however, lighten your mood and raise the vibrations in a space. You might have a different experience with herbal sprays, so don't take my word as the end-all-be-all. Experiment and see how you fare with various cleansing methods.

Another effective method of cleansing is asperging. A common method of asperging is dipping a sprig of rosemary or other fresh herb into blessed water then sprinkling it around your space. Any sprig of herb will work including rosemary, lavender, pine, cedar, or bay. What water you use is up to you. I like using moon water that I've collected on the Full or Waning Moon. Or blessed water, which is simply water that I've asked my gods to bless with their fierce, protective energy. You might also choose to cleanse your space by some other method first, then asperge your space in dedication to your gods or guides as sort of a "christening" or house blessing.

While witches embrace the darkness, we also know that negative entities hide in the dark. As do secrets. If it's been a while, open the blinds and curtains and let the sunlight in.

Have you ever been in a home with palpable negative energy with all the blinds shut? I get that instinctive urge to throw the windows open and let the air and light back in. Sure, the sunlight might not be enough to rid your home of a troubled spirit, but it's at least enough to raise the vibrations and lift the mood.

Same goes for opening the windows – allow a cool breeze to blow in on a nice day. Sometimes all that's needed to shake up stale energy in a home is the air element. I've even used the wind to cleanse myself on especially windy days.

Warding and Sealing

Once you've cleaned and cleansed your home, that's it, right? Wrong. First, one cleansing ritual isn't enough to keep the chaotic energy, entities, and illness at bay forever. Regular cleansings are necessary to keep the energy flowing. In addition, the act of cleansing doesn't protect your home from spiritual intrusion. Warding and sealing do. This is the act of setting up a spiritual barrier that also serves as a sort of magical alarm system. Your wards and seals will not only warn enemies to keep their distance and stay out, but they also alert you on a spiritual level if something is trying to penetrate your shields.

Warding is the spiritual act of guarding your space and yourself from spiritual attacks, illness, entities, and more. Have you ever seen lion statues sitting atop pillars at the end of a mansion's driveway? The stone lions are wards. The lions silently tell outside beings, including humans and spirits, that they will protect this home. And they warn intruders of potential consequences. Placing lions and other predatory animal statues to guard one's property is an old tradition that most people don't even know was once a form of warding.

You can set two lions or other guardians at your front door or end of your driveway or do something else. There are many ways to ward off unwanted spirits. One of my favorite ways to ward is to charge four magical objects then bury them at the four corners of the property. My old school Christian grandmother says angels should be placed at the four corners of your property to ward off evil. But you can use anything you feel is up to the task.

Certain stones are protective including black tourmaline, black obsidian, tiger's eye, bloodstone, hematite, and clear quartz. In addition, metals like iron and steel make great warding devices. Iron is traditionally used to ward off malevolent undead and trickster faeries. But keep in mind, if you use iron as a ward, you'll likely deter many types of faeries.

Other wards to consider may already be in your yard. You can draw or paint protective symbols on natural rocks and branches while infusing with intention. I frequently use powerful runes like Algiz, Tiwaz, Ansuz and Thurisaz for warding purposes. Hagstones make great warding stones, as they are traditionally known to protect your home from illness and intrusion. There are certain types of plants and trees that also act as wards. You can grow these in your yard, garden, or in pots on the front doorstep.

How to Perform a Warding of Your Property and Home
This is one of the most important magical acts you can do to protect your home and family. Warding your property is a compelling way to tell the spiritual world that you mean business. That you won't tolerate unwanted intruders, spiritual attack, or misfortunes to befall your household. Your wards erect a barrier in the ether that encircles your property with a protective force.

Please note, if you live in a space where you don't have access to the grounds or property, for example an apartment or a single room, modify this ritual to meet your needs. My suggestion is to place four wards in the corners of your room or apartment (inside is fine) that you can conceal from others (if need be). Instead of stones or runes, consider placing four plants (real or fake) in the four corners and burying your wards in the pots. Or place guardian statues around your room or apartment which can be charged with protective energy. You can even place petition papers under each statue. AND infuse each statue with a protective herbal brew. The options are endless. Let your intuition and creativity guide you.

Oh, and before I forget, this ritual can be pretty messy. There are herbs, oils, and dirt involved.

What You'll Need:

- 4 Warding Objects: choose 4 stones, runes, iron pieces, small protective statues, shells, etc.
- 3 Protective Herbs, for example: rosemary, sage, thorns, angelica, agrimony, pepper, cayenne, etc. (about a tablespoon of each is plenty. It can be fresh or dried)
- Oil: olive, sunflower, avocado, peanut, etc. (you'll need about a cup's worth or less. Use what you have on-hand)
- Mortar and Pestle (or bowl and spoon)
- Medium plate or container (fill this with your oil. The opening needs to be large enough that you can place your warding objects into it)
- Small shovel
- Small cup of water (as offering)

What to Do:
1. Gather your ingredients.
2. Cleanse your space and supplies (no need to cleanse the herbs).
3. Set the witchy mood (via music, incense, candlelight) and enter a mental space where you are focused, relaxed and open to the Ether.
4. Raise the cup of water and offer it to Spirit (whatever spirits or energies you work with, i.e., pagan gods, the Universe, spirit guides, familiars, angels, etc.)
5. Next, take one of your chosen herbs and tell it its job. For example, "I call on you, sage spirit, to ward off evil entities that come near my home." Then place it in your mortar or bowl.
6. Repeat step number 5 for the other two chosen herbs.
7. With your pestle or spoon, gently mix the 3 protective herbs together and say, "by root, earth, and stone, protect my home. Protect my home. Protect my home." Repeat this 3 times but up to 13 times only ending with an odd number.
8. Tell the oil what its job is, "oil smooth and slick, I call on you to adhere these protective herbs to my wards."
9. Add your protective herbs to the oil in your plate/container.
10. Now, take your 4 warding devices, one at a time, and submerge them in the herb-infused oil. This act quenches each ward in the extra protective energies of the herbs and oil. If they're too large to drown completely, roll each ward in the herbed oil so that they are thoroughly drenched.
11. Take your wards and shovel outside.
12. Start at the Northern most corner of your property. Close your eyes while still holding the wards.

13. Take your first ward and bury it in the first corner, chanting whatever you feel deep in your gut or something like, "my home is encircled in a barrier of positive energy. This ward will shield and protect me from illness, misfortune, intruders and evil entities."
14. Walk in a deosil pattern (clockwise), from North to East to South to West, burying one ward at each of the rest of the 3 corners of your property (so that all 4 corners have a ward). Chanting your protective prayer at each corner OR the entire time (do what you feel drawn to do). If you prefer to visualize a protective wall or bubble being built through the process, you may do that too.
15. End at the Northern-most corner and announce, "my home, property, and its inhabitants are safe and sound. My wards act as barbed wire to harmful energies that try to come around. So be it."

One more note on warding four corners of your property – not everyone has a square or rectangular shaped yard. Some folks may have a circular property, oblong, or even triangular. Some have no defined shape. The key is to lay wards around the perimeter of your property. So, if you have a triangular shaped property for example, lay your wards in the 3 corners. If it's circular, you can still lay 4 wards. You get the picture. Do what works.

Sealing

Sealing is like warding but a practice in which you're "locking" negative energy out and "sealing" current positive energy in. My mom and I refer to this practice as sealing because it feels a bit different from warding, but you'll find most witches simply refer to it as warding or as casting protective charms. The act of spiritually sealing your home consists of drawing symbols on doorways, windows, and other entries to the home. OR by drawing a line of salt or protective powder over each threshold.

    I typically seal my windows, doors, and any other entryways at the same time as my warding ritual. My goal is to keep up with this magical maintenance routine once every three months. Or as needed. I say as needed because there will be times when things slip through your wards…this doesn't mean that you failed or didn't cast the wards correctly. It means that it's time to refresh your wards AND potentially consider other methods of protection for your home.

    Sometimes we can do everything right and spirits still slip through. This is often due to other individuals in your home bringing energies into the house. But can also be a result of renovations on an older house, new pets, traumatic events on the land such as local fires or floods, or any other number of reasons. I've found that if I do all three (cleansing, warding and sealing) at once, the barrier protecting my house from spiritual energies is strongest. But, like I said, there will be times when you notice something is amiss. Sometimes your wards act as alarms, and they'll alert you that something has slipped past the goalie. So technically, wards work in two ways. They keep things out and warn us when things are trying to come in.

    Back to sealing your home. The easiest way to do this is to dip your finger in oil and go from room to room, drawing protective symbols and words on every entry/exit. This means all doors to the outside world, windows, exhausts, and chimneys. I perform this ritual in the same way as warding, but I start at my front door. Then I move clockwise through each room and end at my front door. Don't forget your chimneys and exhausts! These are important entry-points for spirits that people forget to magically seal. Why do you think

Santa comes down the chimney and not in the front door? As you draw each symbol, visualize these symbols as spiritual "locks" that keep negative energy out. Knock, knock. Who's there? Bad energy. Stay the 'eff out.

Another way to seal your home is to follow the same directions above, but instead, spread a protective powder over each threshold. This means drawing a line with the powder from left to right over doorways and windowsills. Powerful, warding powders I've used include salt, witch's black salt, red brick dust, black pepper, cayenne powder, eggshell powder and other mixes with multiple herbs and ingredients. Use what you have on-hand. Herbs in your own yard work wonders, including chickweed, rose petals, vines, oak leaves, etc.

Home Protection Powder Recipe & A Sealing Ritual
What You'll Need:

- Rosemary: for protection
- Rue: for banishing and exorcism (strong warding properties)
- Basil: for prosperity and purification
- Bay: for increasing intuition (being able to sense threats)
- Thorns cut from the bush (rose, honey locust, cactus, bougainvillea, etc.): for warding.
- Salt: for warding, purification
- Mortar and pestle: the tool you'll use to mix it all together.

What to Do:

1. Blend all ingredients together in a mortar and pestle. If you don't have these ingredients or you grow your own herbs, substitute for what you do have.

2. While you're blending, activate the ingredients. Tell them what their job is.
3. Then spread the home protection powder across your thresholds (in the doorframes, fireplaces and windowsills) starting at the front door, moving clockwise around the house. Then ending at the front door.
4. When you spread the powder over each threshold, spread it from left to right and pray over it each time.
5. Once you've ended back at your front door, say something like, "by the power of my ancestors, gods and guides, this home is sealed from negative forces and invites only the Divine. So be it."

Protective Charms

In addition to your magical protection rituals, you might feel drawn to place protective charms around your home. Charms can be anything you feel provides a means of spiritually warding off negativity. Almost every culture, religion, and family have their own protective charms, whether they call them "charms" or not. Christians use crosses, the images of Jesus, Mary, and the Saints. You might find the Nazar amulet hanging from your Persian neighbor's window. Or lion statues at your grandma's front door. You might even notice your local courthouse has a symbol on the outside of the building. All symbols carry power – even company logos!

Protective charms are powerful for a few reasons. One, because *you believe* they have power. And two, because they literally give off that energy. You'll hear a lot of witches tell you "It's all about your intentions" and "the magic is in you, not in the tools". And while I agree your intentions are crucial to the outcome of any magical working, magic is more than just intentions. Otherwise, what's the point in using all those awesome herbs, tools, and crystals? This is my opinion, of course, and others will disagree. And *you* may even disagree, and that's okay too. But in my experience, tools, herbs, crystals, and other spell ingredients have their own energies they lend to my workings of which helps my spells and rituals manifest the desired results. Otherwise, I'm just holding a bowl full of herbs and a kitchen knife for the heck of it. As mere props in a play. Yes, I think it's about your own personal power and belief, BUT witches also acknowledge the innate power in the world around them. That also applies to the tools and ingredients we use in our spells. Which means these things are more than just toys.

Now for the fun. Hanging charms anywhere near or on your front door is a solid line of defense. Thread a red ribbon through a hag stone and hang on or next to the door to ward off evil. Hang a witch's broom above the door or set it next to the door bristles up. If the bristles are touching the floor, be prepared for bad luck. Hanging a horseshoe above the door wards off trickster faeries and bad luck. Point it upwards, so that the horseshoe forms a U shape. Otherwise, if your prongs are down, your luck will "run out" and spirits will run in. The Irish side of my family has employed this protective charm for centuries. My mother still hangs one above her front door and barn door too.

Literally any objects or tool that feels protective to you may be used as a charm to protect your Otherworldly Household. The troll cross from Sweden can be worn or hung above one's bed to ward off nightmares, malevolent faeries and astral entities. Any symbol that represents your gods, guides, or ancestors may be charged with their energy and placed around the home. For example, a small owl figurine that was my late great grandmother's now sits on my altar. Its gaze guards my space and family.

Witch's bells should be hung on the front or back door and in places you feel require extra warding power. I have a set of bells that hang from my armoire door. Inside is an entire shrine dedicated to my ancestors, guides and gods. The bells act as a warding device and prevent unwanted spirits from trying to come out of the mirror or armoire. It is, after all, over a hundred and fifty years old. Who knows what lies just beyond.

Spell bags filled with herbs, roots, stones, and other items can be hung from doorknobs, nails on walls, bookshelf hooks, placed under pillows and mattresses, stuffed in drawers, and anywhere else you feel is necessary. I often add protective herbs like rosemary, pepper, juniper, rose thorns, and sage to a muslin bag along with salts, powders, nails, and other warding devices. Then I lay the bag on my altar and ask my gods to charge it with battle energy. I also put these spell bags in my vehicle, and I carry them in my purse while traveling abroad.

If you're experiencing a bout of nightmares, sleep paralysis and night terrors, you may be the victim of psychic attack. If this is the case, try placing black tourmaline under your bed. A bowl or cup of water under the bed is said to "soak up" negativity. A piece of red cord or string can be tied to your bedpost to ensure your astral body returns to your physical body every night.

Images, paintings, and photographs of your guardians, guides, ancestors, and animal allies may be hung all around the home for protective purposes. There's no limit to the charms that you choose. I've even read of people inscribing runes on their windowsills and above their doorways. Placing mirrors in windowsills outwards to reflect any negative energy is always effective. And don't forget the good ol' fashioned witch bottle.

The Traditional Witch Bottle

Witch bottles are one of the key pieces in witchcraft history that we have archaeological evidence of. Clay and glass jars and vessels have been found in England and the United States from centuries past. Historians are able to correctly identify these artifacts based on their contents: pins, needles, nails, broken glass, wood, fabric, human effects (fingernail clippings, hair, bone, teeth, urine, etc.) and sometimes herbs and stones. Witch bottles are buried in the earth near the front door of a home, under the hearth, or somewhere on the property.

One of the main purposes of a witch bottle is protection from evil spirits, curses and dark magic. Why would someone need protection from evil spirits and curses? In the old days, people believed witches were everywhere and that they were the cause of all that went wrong: illness, injury, a poor harvest, bad weather, etc. When folks felt like they were the target of a witch's sorcery, their defense was to counteract with their own magic. A witch bottle was frequently used for this very reason.

We know how powerful these bottles are and their uses, but HOW do they work? From a modern witch's perspective: human personal effects like fingernail clippings, hair, a person's piece of clothing and bodily fluids is put in witch bottles to attract the spirit to the intended victim. It tricks the spirit into believing the victim is inside the bottle. Then, when the spirit or magic enters the bottle, the pins, nails and sharp objects penetrate and capture it. By burying the witch bottle, the spirit trapped in the bottle will be "grounded" or put to rest by the earth itself.

How to Make Your Own Witch Bottle

Warning: This traditional spell isn't necessarily the "fluffy bunny" type of witchcraft. Just a warning, when you cast this spell, the heebie jeebies might be a legitimate part of the experience. Remember, witchcraft isn't always pretty, no matter what you see on Instagram, but it's not about the aesthetic…it's about the POWER inside waiting to be released.

What You'll Need:

- a sturdy glass bottle or jar with lid
- an odd number of sharp objects to "snag" the spirit: pins, nails, needles, broken glass, etc.
- personal effects: hair (find on a pillow or hairbrush), nail clippings, teeth, small piece of clothing, etc.
- urine
- small black candle (a candle that's NOT in a holder – chime candle is best)
- lighter/matches
- shovel

How to Make It:

A word before you begin, remember to focus on your intention the ENTIRE time.

1. Gather your ingredients and prepare your space. Prepare your mind.
2. Put the pins or sharp objects and personal effects into the bottle.
3. Add urine over the pins and personal effects. Yes, this is the gross part, but TOUGHEN UP, WITCH!
4. Cap the bottle with the lid.
5. Burn the black candle on top of the bottle. The fire is activating or heating up the spell inside. Don't leave

the candle unattended. Allow the candle wax to spill down onto the lid. The wax seals your intentions and energy inside. Burn the candle all the way down.
6. OPTIONAL STEP: you can "heat up" the bottle again by holding it over an open fire. This step adds more power to your spell but isn't required since you've already burned a candle on top.
7. Dig a hole on your property deep enough for your bottle to be buried entirely. Its best by the front door OR by your bedroom window. However, if you can't bury it there, anywhere on the property will do, as long as it's not at risk of being dug up.
8. Place your witch bottle inside the ground, the entire time visualizing malevolent spirits being sucked into the bottle and trapped forever.
9. Leave the witch bottle there. Never dig it back up!

Welcoming Protective Spirits and Guardians

Today there are many kinds of witches. Some that believe in gods and all manner of spirits. Some that only believe in the power of the universe and the energies all around us. And even some that claim they are a Christian and a witch and work with God, Mary, the Saints, and angels. Whatever your flavor or tradition of witchcraft is your own. Whatever spirits you choose to work with is totally up to you. If you've read my other book, Modern Witchcraft: A Beginner's No-Nonsense Guide to the Craft, you'll know that I support everyone forging their own paths. The same goes for spirit work. Either you engage or you don't. There's no right or wrong in *your* witchcraft.

I personally have found it beneficial to work with spirits. I am a hard polytheist, which means I believe in multiple gods and goddesses, ancestors, elementals and faeries, familiars, and all types of spirits. I believe they are real and can be communicated with and invited into the Otherworldly Household to guide and protect you and your family. Does this mean all spirits should be summoned into your home? Absolutely not. That would be like throwing your front door wide open and telling everyone that walked by that they could come inside and stay awhile. There are certain spirits and energies that will align with you and your family and others that will not. Again, this is going to be up to you to decide which spirits you invite into your home.

The first line of spiritual defense, in my experience, is my ancestral guides. We all have ancestors that look out for us. You have certain ancestors who are watching over you right now, ensuring your safety. That is their duty. Your ancestral guardians may have been warriors, soldiers, bodyguards, police officers, knights, shieldmaidens, mercenaries, gladiators or protective parents. They're not difficult to find and communicate with. Put out that spiritual beacon – light a candle and ask your ancestral guardian to come forth. The candleflame serves as a signal to the spirit world. When you speak your invitation, clearly state that your ancestral guardians who are well in spirit are welcome in your home.

Then comes your animal guardian spirits. Every witch has at least one animal guardian spirit. Sometimes witches employ these spirits as familiars, but often these animal spirits are with us from birth. In opposition to the familiar spirit who requires a contract, the animal guardian spirit does not. I've found they are the quickest to respond in times of need, second only to your ancestral guardians.

Following your ancestors and animal guardian spirits is your personal gods and goddesses. Some gods are not in the business of protecting us, while others jump at the chance. Other gods expect us to defend ourselves. It depends on your situation and the gods you work with. For instance, one of my goddesses is well known for being a protector of women and children. And she has done exactly that for me and my children. But Loki isn't so much excited about protecting me as he is teaching me hard lessons. Therefore, you may find that one of your gods is there often to protect you, while others are in your life for other (just as important) reasons.

Again, who you choose to call into your space is your business. If you choose to only ask the universe and positive energy to shield your home from harm, I've heard this works a charm too.

How do you invite protective spirits into your Otherworldly Household? First, you already have your ancestral and animal guardian spirits with you. There's no need to invite them in. But as far as other spirits like gods and elementals, my suggestion is to make sure you've cleaned, cleansed, and decluttered your space first. I also HIGHLY recommend warding and setting up protective charms before invocation. This way you'll filter out the negative spirits when you invite in the positive. Then set up sacred space, which means a shrine or altar of some kind. It doesn't have to be elaborate. Even something as small as a little tray on your kitchen counter with your guide's image and a small offering cup. Or as large as a China hutch completely dedicated to your spirits.

Next, set out offerings for those you plan to invite in. And what I do next might not be for everyone, but I find it sets the tone and symbolically does the trick. Typically, I perform this small ritual at night. I light a white candle, open my front door, and shine the candle into the threshold. Then

I say, "Loki, Fire Bringer, Laufey's son, Great Creator Spirit, I welcome you into my home and ask that you dwell in my sacred space in peace and harmony with the rest of my family. To work with me in my household exclusively. May this light guide you in and give you my warmest of welcomes." Obviously, if you don't work with Loki, then you'll make this prayer about the spirit you choose to invite in.

It is imperative that you've done your research before inviting a spirit into your home. You wouldn't invite a stranger into your home and give them a room free of rent, would you? Don't do it with spirits either. Do your research first. Consider: is this a spirit you've met in meditation and with whom you felt loving vibes? Does this spirit hound you for offerings or make you feel drained? Does this spirit give you nightmares or good dreams? One of the first lessons in spirit work is learning how to vet out the spirits who don't have your best interest at heart versus those that do. If you're not sure, don't open your front door. Whatever you summon, you must also know how to banish.

Also be sure you understand what these spirits like and dislike. For instance, if you're invoking a Celtic faery goddess like Cliodhna, she's not a big fan of fire and smoke. So, if you have her altar lit up with candles and you have herb bundles smoking around your house, she might take a peek in and peace out. Instead, coax her in with an essential oil diffuser or with a simmer pot bubbling on the stove. She's more of a watery, earthy spirit over fire and air. That's just one example. Also consider if the wards you've laid would drive off the spirit you're now trying to invoke. For example, and I'll use Cliodhna again, if you've placed iron in the four corners of your property, she might pass by and even be irritated. Iron is to (most) faeries what kryptonite is to Superman.

Once your protective spirits are at home, regular maintenance of these relationships is necessary. This means speaking to your spirits, providing them occasional offerings, meditating, and asking them for messages and dreams. Divining with cards, runes, bones, and charms to speak to your spirits and accept their guidance. Even keeping a page or more for each spirit in your grimoire.

Chapter 3

Household Spirits

In the last chapter, we discussed invoking protective spirits into the Otherworldly Household. In this chapter, we'll focus on the various household spirits that might already be in your home AND a few of the popular deities and faeries historically associated with the witch's home.

Household Gods and Goddesses

Through the centuries, nearly every culture has had some sort of kitchen or hearth god they've worshiped. Sometimes these deities were worshiped in an entire region, sometimes they were specific to the town or family itself. Let's meet some of them.

Bes, Egyptian God of the Home

Ancient Egyptians, particularly women and children, loved the hearth god Bes. Bes is the dwarf-like protector of mothers and children and is also a guardian of musicians, dancers, and prostitutes. During the New Kingdom era, Bes was tattooed on thighs of dancers and prostitutes alike. His image was frequently placed over doorways and hearths to protect the household and its inhabitants from evil.

Brigid

One of the most well-known of the Celtic pantheon, Brigid is a triple-goddess of fire, healing, and poetry. Brigid's cult was so prevalent that she's still in Ireland and Scotland today in the form of Saint Brigid. Her holy day is Imbolc, also called Saint Brigid's Day, celebrated on

February 1st in the Northern Hemisphere and August 1st in the Southern Hemisphere. Because she is the goddess of the sacred flame, she is also associated with the hearth-fire. Where there is fire, there is Brigid (the Exalted One).

Cailleach

The Cailleach was a goddess in Scotland in ancient times. She's the old woman of winter. The reason she is sometimes worshiped as a hearth goddess is because she watches over the dormant seeds through the winter months, therefore ensuring a bountiful harvest. What do we do with our harvest? We transform it in our kitchens to nourish our bodies and souls. The Cailleach is generally depicted as a wise old woman, but sometimes she's a hideous hag with a blue-green face and an apron. Often you will see kitchen spirits in this form.

Cerridwen: Goddess of the Cauldron

Cerridwen is a Welsh hearth goddess and the Keeper of the Cauldron. The cauldron, a symbol of wisdom and transformation, was once a key feature at every hearth. One of the elements of the hearth is transformation, because we take food and transform it to feed ourselves and our families. In this way, we honor the hearth and the goddess Cerridwen as one of the Otherworldly Household gods.

Hestia & Vesta

Hestia is an ancient Greek hearth goddess and also a goddess of family and state. She is the virgin daughter of Cronos and Rhea. Her name translates to *hearth* or *altar*, and therefore she was once worshiped as the goddess of the hearth in many ancient Greek households. There were temples dedicated to Hestia, all with a sacred inner hearth that was constantly tended by priests or priestesses. The Roman equivalent of Hestia is Vesta.

Juno: Guardian of Hearth & Home

Juno is a Roman guardian of the home, marriage, and family. Therefore, you may choose to work with her as a hearth goddess. She was a protector of women and had many different names throughout Roman history. Set up an altar in her name in your kitchen or family room and watch the blessings roll in!

Zao Jun: Chinese Kitchen God

Also known as Zao Shen, Zhang Lang, or the Chinese Kitchen God, Zao Jun guards the hearth. He is one of many hearth deities in Chinese folklore and Taoism. The Chinese Kitchen God's job is to watch over the goings-on in the home and report back to the Jade Emperor in Heaven. A family would be rewarded or punished based on what Zao Jun had seen of their deeds in the previous lunar year. Today many Chinese families hang pictures of Zao Jun above their stoves and give various offerings to him throughout the year. Some light firecrackers in his name.

Household Faeries and Elves

Before having Alexa and Google Home devices reminding us of when to complete our chores, there were lucky people who had house faeries who helped with tasks left undone. The house elf finished the leftover cleaning, cooking, and mending. Wouldn't that be nice to have a faery in your home helping you finish your chores while you sleep? Depending on the region, there are different types of house faeries with their own quirky names. Like…

The Scottish House Elf: The Brownie

The most beloved house elf in folklore is the Scottish Brownie. The Brownie is a small male creature, between one and two feet tall, who takes up residence in a deserving family's home. The Brownie originates in Scotland, but some say the Scottish immigrants brought the Brownie with them to the United States and Canada in the seventeen and eighteen hundreds. And, if that's true, you might find them all over the world. The Brownie's temperament is mild, and he is rather helpful with chores around the house.

When the woman of the house goes to bed, the Brownie finishes her chores. He is also helpful on the farm. He brings in firewood and harvest crops, and he is a shapeshifter who shifts into the form of a rooster. He takes this shape, I've heard, just to wake up the house with a good, loud crow in the morning. Others believe the rooster is the Brownie's familiar and crows to tell him when to go to bed (although humans believe the rooster crows to wake us up in the morning). The Mother Goose Rhyme "I Had a Little Rooster" illustrates this fun symbiotic relationship between the rooster and the Brownie.

How to Attract a Brownie

The Brownie enjoys a family who is kind and hard-working and will make himself at home in a warm nook or cranny like an undisturbed cupboard or an incredibly high shelf. Attract him to your home with offerings of bread, honey, sweet cream, cakes, and ale. Folklore says to never give clothing to a Brownie (or any house elf, for that matter) because they will take the gift and leave. JK Rowling uses this bit of lore in her famous series: Harry Potter gives Dobie a sock, thereby granting Dobie his freedom from servitude to the Malfoy family. It is very good luck to have a Brownie living in your house, not just for their help with chores, but because they keep away bad spirits and bring prosperity.

The Bean-Tighe: The "Irish Brownie"

Like the Scottish Brownie, the Irish Bean-tighe (pronounced ban-tee) is a benevolent Irish house faery that cares for a nice family. The main difference between the Brownie and the Bean-tighe is gender. The Bean-tighe is a small, elderly female creature who wears tattered, old-fashioned dresses and has a wrinkled face. Her name *Beantighe* (*ban-tee*) translates to "woman of the house and sounds an awful lot like the *Beansidhe* (*banshee*). Both faeries are linked to the oldest of Irish families. But, in opposition to the ominous Beansidhe, the Beantighe is friendly and warm. She is a housekeeper and will watch over the animals and children.

The Bean-tighe loves a warm fire and kind-hearted humans, and she will watch over the children at night. Irish folklore tells of mothers getting up in the middle of the night to check on the children and found the children had an extra blanket covering them or a window open/closed to adjust the temperature in the room. This was the work of the Bean-tighe. The Bean-tighe loves cream and berries, and therefore should be offered such.

Other tales tell of old Irish women who were careful not to keep their homes too clean, for fear of being accused of having a Bean-tighe. During the Witch Trial era, if you were thought to be a friend of the faeries, you were often accused of witchcraft. If you are of Milesian descent, the Bean-tighe will be more likely to take up residence in your home, but she has been known to help those who call to her.

You will hear from some self-proclaimed "faery experts" that the beantighe is not a house faery. And that there's no real proof that she is. I counter with, is there proof that ANY faery actually exists? Or what they look like and how they act? The beantighe is, in fact, mentioned in old Irish folklore. I believe people and families passed her down in oral tradition, more so than in written, and so it's difficult to track down complete resources on her. I first learned of her in Edain McCoy's book A Witch's Guide to Faery Folk[1]. And then I met her on the astral plane. Reach out to her, if you feel called to do so, and see for yourself. Just because one person doesn't believe in a faery doesn't mean you should follow suit.

The Boggart: The Naughty House Elf

The Boggart is a Scottish house elf that you might not want in your home. His other names are hobgoblin, goblin, boogie man, bogey and gob. Boggarts look like a distorted, mangled Brownie. Some believe he is a Brownie gone bad. Folklore says if you have a Brownie in your home and don't treat him well, he will turn into a Boggart. Boggarts eat the wood in the walls, roof, and floors, like a large termite, and they will destroy the foundation of a home if not exorcised. Another theory is the Boggart is a relative of the Ballybog (a faery that guards the peat bogs). The Boggart is known to torment the household with an interest in picking on the children. They will steal the food off a child's plate and try to smother them in their sleep. This is likely where the concept of the Boogieman originated.

Bwbachs: The Welsh Cottager Faery

Bwbachs (pronounced boo-box) are Welsh solitary house faeries that live in Welsh cottages. They are protective of the house; however, they don't help with chores and can become a nuisance. Their mischievous nature leads them to chase off anyone who they feel threatens the household, which might include friendly neighbors, close friends, and

---

[1] See bibliography at end of book for full reference.

even family members. They manifest as tiny men wearing red hats and loincloths. Keep the bwbachs happy by leaving food offerings (traditionally bread) and by keeping the house warm. To distract them from pestering your house guests, keep the milk and bread out and stoke up the fire. Other names for bwbachs are cottagers and booakers. I hope I reincarnate as one of these guys.

The Monaciello

House faeries are traditionally known to enjoy a good drink and wine is no exception. The Monaciello is an Italian house faery who enjoys alcohol so much that he will move into a well-stocked wine cellar. A half-stocked wine cellar will do, if he doesn't have a better option. He will protect your wine cellar when given a bit of the wine regularly. The name *Monaciello* means "*little monk*" because he is small and wears a monk's hood. The Monaciello is always drunk, but he is usually friendly. He's a happy drunk. Folklore says the Monaciello guards the wine cellar, but his secret is that he is also guarding a treasure. If you can steal the Monaciello's hood, you get his treasure.

The Clurichaun

The Clurichaun is a cousin of the Irish Leprechaun. He looks exactly like the Leprechaun except he wears red instead of green. And he lives in human abodes instead of in caves or hollows. He drinks a lot of wine and lives in wine cellars; however, he is never sloppy and always well-groomed. The Clurichaun's job, of which he's taken upon himself, is to supervise the wine cellar and ensure there are no leaks nor a skunked wine stock. Give him a drink regularly, and he will remain happy and friendly. Ignore or mistreat him and he will empty your wine bottles and leave your cellar in disarray. If you hear a jaunty Irish tune coming from the wine cellar, you might have a Clurichaun on premises.

The Kobold: A German House Elf

Like the Scottish brownie, the Kobold is a German sprite who helps with the house chores. The name *Kobold* has a few translations, my favorite translation being "the one who rules the house". Kobolds are short, ugly men with large ears, hairy bodies, and giant, bulbous noses. They wear a cloak or a suit and a large-brimmed hat. Unlike Brownies, Kobolds love being praised for their work and love being showered with gifts. And they particularly like receiving packages of clothing and food. In comparison to the Brownie, the Kobold will turn into a mischievous or downright malevolent creature if he feels he isn't appreciated. Never make fun or insult the Kobold. Lest you wind up with a plate full of frogs on the dinner table!

The Lares

The ancient Romans honored their household spirits and called them Lares. Each household maintained an altar for these spirits. For prosperous families, there were statues to represent the household's Lares and offerings were left at their feet. The Lares' images were also placed at the dinner table to partake in the family meal. The Lares are guardian spirits who protect the home and family from illness and invasion.

Lares weren't strictly household guardians, but also guardians of natural places, as well as of entire communities. This leads us to believe Lares were originally land spirits (also called *Genius loci*) that were brought into the home and eventually deified. Interestingly, the Lares were frequently portrayed as snakes and were believed to live under the hearth. Perhaps these types of Lares were fire elementals of some kind?

How a House Acquires Its Spirits

Our ancient ancestors believed everything in nature had consciousness. When trees were cut down and used to build a home, the faeries and spirits who lived in the trees were brought into the home by means of transference. Others believed the faeries occupying the landscape where a home was built became household spirits. The land on which to build a home had to be just right. There were many superstitions involving the choosing of the land. For example, our Scandinavian ancestors stayed the night at a site to see if evil spirits manifested. If the person slept peacefully, the home was built there. If he didn't, they would move on and find another place to build.

There were other seemingly logical methods of picking a suitable site, including surveying the ground and nearby trees for signs of a previous fire or flood. Fire was a bad sign, associated with evil spirits, and our ancestors might have refrained from building somewhere that had signs of a fire. And, in some stories, if the individual met a benevolent faery on the site, he would ask the faery to take up residence in the new home and become the household spirit.

Ancestors at the Hearth

Other methods of acquiring a household spirit were more disturbing. In ancient Eastern Europe and parts of Western Asia, when a new home was built, they would sacrifice someone and bury him or her in the walls or under the hearth. The sacrificial spirit would then be eternally tied to the home and became the household god and guardian. When a family member died a violent death in the home, the windows were opened immediately to let the soul out. They didn't want a violent spirit lingering and wreaking havoc on the household. I'm not quite sure why the sacrificial spirit would be happy stuck in the walls for centuries, though. This gives a whole new meaning to those random knocks in the walls at night, doesn't it?

If a family moved into a home that had already been built, the original (now deceased) owner of the home was thought to become the household spirit. Ancestors who lived in a house before their descendants could also become household spirits. Even if you're not living in a house passed down through your family, you can still invite your ancestors into your home to become part of your household's horde of Otherworldly spirits. By maintaining an ancestral altar at the hearth, you honor those who came before you and keep your bloodline's fire aflame.

Your House's Spirit

Have you ever heard your house speak? That groan, creak, and pop in the middle of the night, well, it's not the "house settling". It's your house talking. In older times, our ancestors believed the home had its own consciousness and its own spirit. One that could be appeased through offerings, appreciation, and regular communication. Your house's spirit is unique from your household gods and faeries. It's the literal soul of your home – the energy that came from the wood, stone, brick, and metal that went into the construction of your home. It may also be the spirit of the land underneath the very foundation of your home.

To connect with the spirit of your house, simply start speaking to it. First, give it a name. It was tradition in the old days to name your home and property. Think of the classic novel Anne of Green Gables. Their farm was named Green Gables. And in giving your home a name, you're permitting it to have its own personality. To make itself known to you, your family, and visitors (if you want).

After you've named your home, talk to it whenever possible. Like it's a family member sitting right next to you on the sofa. Don't worry. You can wait until your actual family members aren't around if you're worried what they'll think. Say goodbye before a long trip and address it directly when you return. Thank your house's spirit for keeping you and your loved ones safe from intruders, harsh weather, the elements and illness. Thank it for the blessings its bestowed upon you. I also give an offering to the house's spirit itself if renovations will soon occur.

Feeding Your Household Spirits

If you have ancestors already present, it may be best to set up an altar for them and provide offerings daily or weekly there. This feeds their spirit and shows your gratitude. While ancestors will always protect us whether we care for them or not, if we put in more effort, their blessings for us will amplify. As for feeding/caring for household spirits like Brownies, Bwbachs, and Kobolds, research what offerings they like best traditionally. What each house faery likes could be drastically different from the next.

Room for House Faeries

Ancestors are fond of altars, but household faeries prefer a cozy, private space. You can create a "room" for them in a linen closet or a quiet cabinet or drawer. Clean the space thoroughly and put a small pillow, blankets, and comfy items there for your household faery to rest. Guardian spirits will reside in a doll, statue, bottle or other vessel if invited. Once they've taken up residence in a figure or vessel, clean it regularly, dress it in oils, and give offerings to it. The Slavic

Domovoi may prefer sleeping in a chimney or old wood stove. Keep it clean and uncluttered for him or her.

Chapter 4

Magical Themes and Colors

Before we dive deep into each room, let's talk about themes and colors. The Otherworldly Household will have a decorative theme and vibe that reflects its owner's personal flavor of magic. My advice is this – don't pigeon-hole yourself into just one theme for the entire house if you don't want to. Go on sites like Pinterest and let yourself be inspired by the home décor aesthetics there.

My Otherworldly Household is your average one-story home in the suburbs. Built in 1980. Nothing super witchy about it. But that didn't matter to me. I've made it my magical home with love and with my own personal style. I use the four elements as a major theme in my home, with a smattering of rustic farmhouse pieces. I recommend using your interior design preferences to guide your witchy decorating.

Magical Décor Themes

- **The hedge witch's home**: houseplants everywhere, a big herb garden, a hedge of roses or bushes around the property, wildlife, and animal decor (paintings on the wall, statues, throw blankets, etc.) This theme can be rustic or cottage style.
- **The modern witch's sacred space**: essential oil diffusers, light palette of colors (light gray, white, pastels), houseplants, crystals in every room, tapestries, and a meditation space
- **The cottage witch's home**: a kitchen full of magical tools, a kitchen altar, herbs in the windowsills and on the kitchen counter, possibly a shabby chic (see more

below) or antique theme for furniture, super comfy sofas, and chairs. And your sweetest kitty cat sitting in a rocking chair. A place where you can grab a book and a cuppa and curl up by the fire.

- **The retro witch's home**: antiques from your preferred era or decade, colors to fit your favorite period (rust orange, mustard yellows, and olive green for the 1970's; pink, pastel yellow and light blue for the 1950's; red and light blue for the 1940's, etc.); lace or linen curtains in the kitchen, an ice box and pie safe in the kitchen.
- **Bohemian Theme**: I've noticed caravans of witches gravitate towards the Bohemian home decorating theme. Vibrant colors, intricate embroidery, and Moroccan-inspired designs entice the hippie witch at heart.
- **Shabby Chic**: witches that prefer a feminine, farmhouse or antique style love the shabby chic theme. Pinks, whites, and pastel colors define the shabby chic theme. Floral patterns are witchy and shabby chic, as is distressed furniture, white wicker and cast-iron furniture.
- **Celestial**: this theme reminds me of something you'd see a fortune teller living in. Or an astrologist. Dark colors like black and navy blue mimic the night sky, embellished with gold and shimmery stars, planets, suns, and moons. Great for astrology-loving, cosmic witches from another planet
- **Victorian**: you can go gothic with the Victorian look or just keep it true Victorian style. Either way, many witches associate the Victorian period with being "witchy". It's mysterious and classic. Antiques go a long way with the Victorian theme. Gothic witches love this theme.

- **Rustic (or Farmhouse):** I love this theme! It reminds me of my childhood home. Hardwood floors, apron sink, aprons hanging on the wall, a pie safe in front of the kitchen window. My grandmother had a farmhouse style home and I thought it was perfectly magical! Adapt this to your home. Great for hearth, cottage, and forest witches
- **French Countryside:** like the farmhouse or rustic look but geared more towards what you'd see in the countryside of France. Look it up. You'll love it. Great for cottage and hearth witches.
- **Coastal theme for Sea Witches**: this theme is PERFECT for sea witches. Everything is based on the beach, ocean, and coastal vibes. So, if you live near the beach OR are just a water element person, consider the coastal motif for your witchy bedroom.

Color Magic in the Home

Sure, theme is important when it comes to decorating the witch's Otherworldly Household, but so is your color palette. Think about the color on the walls in each room. Think about the colors of the furniture and decorations. Do these colors match your intentions and each room's purpose? You might find painting your kitchen walls red reminds you of your ancestral hearth-fire and seems to make everyone hungry. But when you put red in the bathroom, it doesn't flow with the water element there and makes people feel irritable and rushed. Maybe a blue palette in the bedroom is relaxing and soothing, but others might find it lacks the "spice" they need in that space.

Before you start filling your Otherworldly Household with new furniture, fancy magical tools and decorative pieces, ensure the colors align with your intentions. Here's a general guide to colors and their magical properties. Look it over and then decide:

Black

Black is a color that polarizes people from different cultures. Some cultures associate black with death and mourning (think what we wear to funerals in America), while others think of black as symbolic of evil. Yet those of us who practice witchcraft know the true power of black. It is mystery and wisdom in one. Black reflects negativity and pulls us deeper. It's great for warding off illness and evil, diving deep into shadow work, and teaches us to question life's mysteries. Interestingly, in some cultures, the color white is the color of death and mourning. Not black.

If you're goth at heart, consider adding black pieces to your home décor. I've even seen witches paint second-hand vanities, hutches, and nightstands pure black. Truly, black is a witchy color and adds that element of mystery and the occult. But, if black doesn't make you feel like the sorcerer you are, don't use it.

White

White is another polarizing color. In America, we view white as a symbol of purity which is why most brides wear white to weddings. Yet in some Eastern cultures, white means death. In Vietnam white is worn to funerals, not weddings. How you incorporate white in your home is up to you. I think too much white is blinding and plain. But some folks fill an entire room with white furniture and walls and feel completely at peace. White's magical properties are purity, protection, connecting with the divine, healing, unity, balance, connection with angels and spirit guides, transformation, and enlightenment.

Brown

Brown might not be everyone's favorite color, but it is as powerful as the rest. It's one of my favorites for home décor, because it's the color of Mother Earth. It represents the soil we walk on and where things grow. It symbolizes the bark and branches of the trees. Use brown in your magic when working with the earth element. Brown's magical properties include animal magic, chthonic deities, grounding and centering, primality, garden magic, tree magic, the Ogham, traveling the World Tree, the harvest, manifestation and Earth protection. Plus, there are SO many shades of brown: tan, chocolate, mahogany, dark, light, etc.

Blue

Everyone in my house loves blue. It's a fan favorite, but why? Blue is the color of the sky, certain flowers, fruits, and of the water. Our veins are blue. This beautiful color's magic properties are healing, peace and harmony, communication (verbal, nonverbal and written), and truth. It's linked to the throat chakra, which makes it powerful in speaking one's truth. And links it to our ears and listening skills. Blue is a quintessential magical color for the bathroom, representing the water element, purification and for soothing frazzled nerves.

Neon and Dark Blues: shades of lapis, royal blue, sapphire, navy blue, etc. Blue is a color with versatility. Each shade arouses a different emotion in the individual. Dark and bright blues have magical properties that include emotional and physical healing, water magic, communication, and astral projection.

Light Blues: shades of cornflower, periwinkle, baby blue, etc. These shades of blue are effective in healing magic and bring a sense of peace and tranquility to chaotic situations. Light blue known as *"haint blue"* has been used in the South for centuries to ward off evil spirits. Some practitioners still paint their porch roofs haint blue to keep the evil out.

Purple

Purple is the color of modern metaphysics. Metaphysical shops frequently incorporate purple in their logos, décor, and furniture. This isn't a coincidence – purple is the official color of magic. Purple also represents royalty, intuition, beauty, and psychic abilities. Specifically, it enhances all clair gifts: clairvoyance (clear-seeing), clairsentience (clear-feeling), clairsalience (clear-smelling), clairaudience (clear-hearing) and clairgustance (clear-tasting). I see it as a lush color and therefore think of all things rich, powerful, and elegant, especially in the Otherworldly Household. If you have an altar or an entire magical room, purple is a powerful color theme. Witches will paint the front door purple to let others know, there's a witch that lives here!

Dark and Neon Purples: grape, violet, royal, wine, indigo, eggplant, etc. Dark and bright purples represent your higher self, royalty, intuition, spiritual power, magic, wisdom, and dreams.

Light Purples: shades of lavender, lilac, orchid, heliotrope and iris. Light and pastel purples mean spiritual healing, relaxation, purification, self-care, and beauty.

Pink

When I was young, I hated pink. Now I'm an adult and it's one of my favorite colors for one specific reason – it represents femininity. For years I fought with my feminine self – I avoided things like self-love, sexual empowerment and honoring my emotions. But pink represents even more than that. It a symbol of friendship, romantic love, and empathy. It's the color of genitalia and therefore of feminine sexuality and creativity. Pink goes well as an accent color in the living room, kitchen, and bedroom.

Neon and Dark Pink: shades of hot pink, fuchsia, punch, shocking pink, and magenta. Neon and dark shades of pink represent female empowerment, radical self-love, and healing of childhood and emotional wounds, platonic love, and friendship.

Light Pink: shades of pastel pink including bubblegum, flamingo, blush, and baby pink. Decorate and embellish with light pink to evoke a sense of femininity, encourage friendship, compassion, gentility, healing of feminine bodily parts (think breast cancer awareness) and protection of the children and home.

Red

Red incites strong emotional reactions. It's often a polarizing color. I've literally seen friends throw down over whether red was a good color. To the positive, red is an energizing color, igniting one's passions. And to the negative, in a state of anxiety or anger, it might push those experiencing these emotions over the proverbial edge. Use red wisely within the home. Red's magical properties include active protection, passion, anger, blood, ancestor work, love, lust, and motivation.

In my old home, we painted the kitchen walls red. And found that somehow it promoted appetite in the little ones. Add red to your bedroom to kick up the romance a notch. Be careful how much though! Too much may draw out anger in some individuals. If you're a fire sign, you might be more likely to decorate with a red palette.

Orange

Orange is a magical color linked to the sacral chakra and therefore a powerful color for creativity of all kinds. In rooms where I've incorporated orange, it increases energy and vitality. It's also useful to boost your inspiration and determination to finish long term projects. And it draws new opportunities your way. Orange's magic properties include attraction, vitality, fertility, and adaptability. Adding orange to workspaces like offices, dens, and study areas is a magical way to boost productivity. It's also helpful in the bedroom to increase fertility, for those who are trying to conceive. Throw some orange sheets or blankets on your bed and BOOM.

Yellow

Yellow is linked to the Sun and to the solar plexus. It raises energy, boosts confidence and self-esteem. Yellow's magical properties are wisdom, intellect, imagination, inspiration, confidence, immortality, growth, joy, communication, and career success. It can be helpful when breaking through negative thought patterns. It is also linked to the air element. Add splashes of yellow to the home office and children's bedrooms. I also have yellow in my dining room to promote joy and discussion during family meals.

Neon and Dark Yellow: sunshine, dandelion, and bumblebee yellow. What do you think of when you see these bright colors? The sun, honeybees, yellow tulips, dandelion heads…all things cheery and bright! Shades of bright yellow are great for magic that brings joy and energy. Moreover, it can also be used to align and balance your solar plexus. Neon yellow acts as a warning sign to predators and on road signs to warn of potential danger. Therefore, it might be helpful to paint the exterior of your home a shade of yellow as a form of protection magic. Or maybe just the shutters?

Light Yellow comes in shades of egg, custard, and banana yellow. When yellow is a pastel shade, it represents the same magic as neon yellow, but with a calm undertone. Don't need a huge BURST of energy but maybe just a tad? Use pastel yellows instead of neon. Also great for gentle communication, new friendship, new opportunity, success, and mental clarity.

Green

What witch doesn't love green? Green is the color of the earth: plants, trees, herbs, algae, lichen, and moss. It's the color of the heart chakra and symbolizes unconditional love. Green's magical properties include love, Mother Earth, abundance, growth, resurrection, youth, good luck, health, connection to the faeries and earthly gods, as well as balance. We have an abundance of green in our living room to promote prosperity and love within the family unit. Plus, I associate the living room with the earth element, so it just made sense to me to decorate with a green palette.

Dark and Neon Green: hunter green, moss green, juniper, clover, and basil. When we think of green, we think of Mother Earth in all its glory. Dark and neon greens are used in money magic, growth, abundance, gardening, healing, love, and more.

Light or pastel greens come in shades of pear, chartreuse, mint, Kelly-green, teal, peridot, and seafoam. Light greens are beneficial for magical rebirth, resurrection, new opportunities, children, fertility, and earth magic.

There is truly no right or wrong when it comes to color and theme in your home. Ignore the trends because they are always changing. One year farmhouse is all the rage, next its shabby chic. Then it changes again. Decorate your home in a way that makes you feel comfortable, joyful, and promotes living a magical life.

Chapter 5

The Witch's Kitchen

I've been practicing kitchen witchery for years, and the first tip I can give you is to transform your kitchen into a magical place where you'll WANT to spend time. Ask yourself this – do you dread being in the kitchen? If the answer is yes, it's time for a witchy makeover. A witch's kitchen shouldn't be a drab, boring space. It should brag about being the heart of the home, filled with satisfying aromas of bread baking in the oven, incense burning on the altar, and tea brewing on the stove. The walls should be covered with enchanted images of herbs, potions, and ancestors. Here, I will teach you how to turn your kitchen into a sacred sanctuary. And a place where you'll want to cook, bake, and make magic.

Quick Ways to Shift the Vibe in Your Kitchen

You don't have to spend a ton of money on creating the picture-perfect Otherworldly kitchen. Sometimes it only takes a small change to shift the entire vibe. Here are some cheap, quick things to try.

Kitchen towels with witchy designs, gothic colors, and Halloween vibes (check out the Dollar Tree, Family Dollar, and other discount stores). Pretty glassware of different colors (these can serve as chalices for offering cups or as decorations. Scour your local second-hand shops). Glass mason jars and canisters filled with herbs, roots, salt, and spices set on the counter or on wall shelves. You'll find mason jars for cheap at Walmart and thrift shops. If you don't want to spend the money, recycle used marinara jars, pickle and olive jars for this purpose. I even save old spice bottles to reuse as spell bottles and to hold small magical curios.

Place a candle and incense burner on the counter or stove. Print out pictures of herbs, food, folk magic, gods and goddesses, ancestors, rustic feasts, etc. from online and frame them. Then hang them on your kitchen wall. Purchase frames for cheap on Amazon or at HomeGoods, OR reuse frames you already have in the house. Take a small pot, some dirt, and a few herb seeds and grow something green in the sunniest part of your kitchen. Or hang bundles of herbs from your pot rack or kitchen curtain rod. A vase with fresh flowers OR faux flowers elevates the mood in any Otherworldly kitchen.

Organization, Purification and Cleanliness

Before you start decorating, it's more important to declutter, clean and organize your kitchen. Decluttering your space allows for positive energy to flow in and old stale energy to flow out. Physically cleaning the kitchen also removes negative energy. Plus, it's just nice to live in a clean, organized space. Isn't it? When my kitchen is clean, I feel free to cook magical meals, bake desserts and breads, and make all kinds of magic…instead of worrying about cleaning. We typically do a deep-clean of our kitchen once every season. This means emptying the pantry, cabinets, and fridge, throwing out old items and wiping everything down. Turn this into a purification ritual by adding a few drops of lemon essential oil to moon water and using this as your cleaning fluid.

After you've cleaned and decluttered your kitchen, it's time to perform a purification ritual. Smoke-cleansing is a good choice, but you can also make a simmer pot. I like to listen to high-vibrational music during purification rituals –

Celtic flutes, Norse drumming, meditation music, and nature sounds. When crafting your simmer pot, choose ingredients with purifying properties like lemons, rosemary, sage, orange and cinnamon sticks. Then save the remnants of the simmer pot and spray it around the kitchen. Taking care of the insides of pantries, cupboards, and cabinets.

Kitchen Altars

Many witches enjoy erecting and tending altars around the home. It gives us a sense of connection with our higher selves and the spirit world. For the kitchen witch, kitchen altars are a place where we honor ancestors, gods, and our household spirits. Your kitchen altar can be as elaborate or as simple as you'd like. A shelf on the wall, the corner of a counter, or an empty cabinet are all appropriate surfaces for your altar. Clean, cleanse and add whatever you feel is appropriate to your altar. My kitchen altar is a wooden tray on which I keep candles, incense, a tiny offering cup, hagstones, Tarot cards, a wolf figurine and small wooden images of Odin and Frigg. When I'm not using it, I place it on top of my fridge to keep it sacred and safe.

Space for Household Spirits and Fae

Some kitchen witches work with household spirits at the hearth. A great way to honor and make household spirits feel welcome is to keep a separate, quiet space for them. Clear a high shelf in the pantry or cabinet. Then add things that would make a household spirit feel right at home: a small bed, dresser, nightstand, books, fireplace, and dishes. Doll furniture works wonders for the household spirit's space. Then invite your household spirit to live there. This is as easy as speaking it into existence, followed by a sweet, homemade treat as an offering. I don't recommend putting anything iron in this space, although I've found iron as a ward to faeries doesn't always apply to kitchen faeries. I wonder if they've built up a tolerance over time.

Kitchen Appliance Magic

It might seem strange that kitchen appliances can also be magical tools. In animism, everything has consciousness and a soul. Staying true to that belief, you'll understand even machines may have consciousness. Why else would we name our vehicles and yell at our precious computers? I imagine what my great great grandparents think of all the convenient tools and appliances I have in my kitchen today, and just how magical they would find them if they were alive. Back in the day, every chore was done by hand, so even a seemingly small chore might have been a large feat. How much more freedom do we have today because of modern advancement? Let's explore how we can use our major kitchen appliances in an Otherworldly way.

The Fridge and Freezer

The refrigerator and freezer are not new concepts, but the ability to plug them in and keep our food ice cold *is* new. Before the freezer was the ice box. Before the ice box, people might have frozen their foods in cold lakes, ponds, creeks, and springs. Using ice in magic isn't new and it can't be claimed by any one magical tradition. This type of magic has likely been used for thousands of years by various cultures. And luckily, we have access to automatic cooling and freezing appliances like the refrigerator and freezer in our Otherworldly kitchens today. When someone tells you you can't use your freezer to cast a spell, tell them to *chill out*.

Freezer spells work in a few ways. Let's examine the magical mechanics, shall we? The freezer's job is simple – to freeze food and liquids. And freezing equals hardening and preservation. Let's say you're working at a job that's become dangerous. A co-worker has made it a hostile environment. You've gone to the boss, but he did nothing to help. You decide to do a binding freezer spell on this coworker. It will work, but don't forget to consider how long you plan to keep the spell going AND how long to keep the spell in the freezer. Once this jerk coworker has either left the job OR left you alone, will you keep their name in your freezer? Or will you wait a certain amount of time, then remove the spell and bury it far off your property? These are important aspects to this type of freezer spell that are worth sorting before casting.

Next, let's say you are at a point in life where something is moving too fast for comfort. And this is causing you significant stress, anxiety, or pain. Is there a way to slow the process down or even stop it in its tracks? Yes. Freezer spells are perfect to do this magical job, as well. And when you're ready to allow the natural timing of this event to flow again, you'll remove the spell from the freezer and let it "defrost". Think of it like this – whatever you want to freeze in place or PRESERVE, your freezer will come in handy.

Most of my research on freezer spells prior to writing this article yielded the same intention – to bind a person or situation. This is probably the most popular intention for a freezer spell, but it's not the only magic that can be made in a freezer. When we use the freezer to craft ice spells, another world is opened to us:

- Freezer spells are great to preserve love.
- And friendship
- To preserve a job opportunity or salary
- To stop time from moving too fast
- Preserve one's health.

- Bind a dangerous person or situation from causing harm.
- When using ice in our spells, it promotes stillness.
- Self-Control
- Focus and concentration.
- Learning how to adapt to abrupt change.
- Cooling a "hot" situation off (the refrigerator is better for this depending on the severity of the circumstances)
- Extreme purification
- In god and goddess dedication rituals (particularly of a Northern pantheon originating in colder climates)

I guess at this point, it's time for me to step in and talk about magical morals when it comes to casting binding spells in the freezer. You'll hear a lot of witches say you should never mess with a person's free will. And to leave things to the Universe or gods to work out. But here's the problem with that – sometimes the universe and gods expect *us* to protect *ourselves*. And if we've done everything we can in the physical and still feel threatened, we have our magic to turn to. If binding spells of any kind are against your morals, you don't have to do them. But if you feel the need to protect yourself or others by casting a binding spell, I won't be mad at you. Witchcraft has been used for centuries to liberate the oppressed. Remember that.

Freezer spells are made up of two main ingredients: water/liquid and the freezer itself. But don't forget to experiment with other intuitive ingredients like herbs, flowers, different types of containers, fruit, meat, etc. And experiment with different ways to use the freezer in your magic. The typical freezer spell involves writing a target's name or the situation on a piece of paper, then put it in water and freeze it. Here's a few more creative ways to make magic with a freezer:

- Make ice cubes with edible flowers and herbs inside. Then use those ice cubes in magical potions. This is incredibly fun to do for the Summer Solstice.
- As a kitchen witch, I use the freezer to freeze meals and foods to be eaten at later dates (for example, freeze your hambone from Christmas and make a soup the following Ostara to represent rebirth)
- Turn fun, at-home science experiments with ice from your freezer into kid-friendly spells.
- Use witch's black salt to melt ice (powerful when defrosting a freezer spell AFTER manifestation)
- Make herbal tea cubes or coffee cubes to add to your potions.
- Preserve your garden seeds for next growing season.
- Make aloe vera ice cubes in the Summer to soothe sunburns and bug bites.
- Prep individual magical smoothie packs for a healthy witchy breakfast.

Stove and Oven

The stove and oven serve as the modern version of the ancestral hearth. In centuries past, our ancestors gathered 'round the hearth. The hearth was the center of the home, as it provided life-giving warmth through the Winter season, cooked our food so we could eat without sickness, and brewed our remedies. Today, our stove and oven provide all of these, though many of us don't require its warmth for survival, as we are fortunate to have central heating. As a witch, we can utilize these modern appliances in many magical ways. Obviously, the stove and oven are useful in kitchen witchery: cooking magical meals, baking bread and desserts with intention, concocting herbal spells and remedies, making healing soups, and much more.

Sink and Dishwasher

Would you believe me if I told you the sink and dishwasher are magical contraptions? The sink is a vessel meant to hold water, akin to a large basin. The closest magical tool to a basin is a cauldron. While we're not brewing or cooking things in the sink, we are do use it as a means of holding that life-giving substance and purifier - WATER. And, think of this, when we were babies, we bathed in our parents' and grandparents' sinks. Sometimes we bathe our small pets in the sink. The sink also serves as a tub for cleaning and cleansing kitchen items that double as witchcraft tools. And the dishwasher? Same thing – water is the key element, and this appliance serves as an automatic purifier. You can charge your sink and dishwasher with intentions of purification, giving these appliances the ability to cleanse things *spiritually* and *physically* at the same time.

A Kitchen Witch's Tools

When I first started cooking, I had a limited supply of tools and ingredients. I was young and didn't have the money to equip my kitchen with fancy items. But I didn't let that stop me. So don't let it stop you! If you don't have the money to afford the kitchen witch tools listed here, don't fret. One day you will, so in the meantime, choose more affordable options. And the most important thing? Put YOUR energy and intention into each meal you cook and every remedy you brew. Then it will all turn out fabulous.

Keep in mind, it's taken me fifteen years of cooking and kitchen witchery to acquire the tools below. Each year, ask your significant other or family members to purchase one of these for you as a gift. Find some of these items at secondhand shops or on sale online. Take your time. The right kitchen witch tools will find you. Sometimes in places you least expect.

The Dutch Oven

My favorite kitchen witch tool is my Dutch oven. In fact, I have two. The one I use the most is a fire-engine red Le Creuset. Every time I lug it out of the cabinet, the vibe in my kitchen automatically shifts from mundane to magical. And when I plop the red beast on the stove, my personal vibrations shift. What can you do with a Dutch oven? So much! I use my red Le Creuset make and enchant stews, soups, roasts, homemade bread, mulled wine, and cider.

My other Dutch oven looks more like a cauldron – cast iron with a heavy lid, metal handle and three legs. I purchased it from Target online for only thirty dollars! I use my cast iron cauldron more for my magical practice - to brew unguents and herbal concoctions, to burn loose incense and petition papers. And for involved candle rituals that require multiple candles, herbs, and other materials. The cauldron contains the fire well and acts as a magical circle around the spell.

Instant Pot

For the kitchen witch on the go, the Instant Pot is a dream. The Instant Pot is a pressure cooker that cooks your food at lightning speeds. It cooks rice in five minutes. Whole pot roasts that would usually take 8 hours in a slow cooker take 1-2 hours in the instant pot! I've also made baked potatoes, tamales, soups, stews, macaroni and more. If you love to make magic in the kitchen but don't have a ton of time, the instant pot is your best friend. It also serves as a cauldron.

Tea Kettle and Diffuser

The tea kettle is a helpful magical tool for the kitchen witch. One of my favorite forms of magic is tea magic. The tea kettle as a kitchen tool is quite old, dating back to at least 3500 BC. There's no doubt in my mind that it's been used by witches since its inception. There are basic tea kettles and electric tea kettles. Kettles that whistle or stay quiet. I prefer a kettle on the stove and one that whistles, as I tend to get distracted and sometimes forget I put the kettle on. You can shop for kettles online, at secondhand shops, or wherever is affordable. They come in all different colors too, which you can also align with intentions. My tea kettle is periwinkle blue, which aligns with my intention of brewing healing, comforting teas.

Continuing with the tea talk, if you make your own herbal tea blends, you'll need a tea infuser. There are tea balls for cheap, as well as cup infusers that infuse your hot water with the herbs of your choice then strain them out when poured. This prevents the tea leaves from spilling into your cup. Conversely, if you want to read tea leaves, don't use an infuser as you'll need to allow the leaves to gather at the bottom of your cup when you're done drinking. Purchase tea infusers and diffusers online almost anywhere. Tea magic is versatile and can be used as herbal remedies, spell potions, floor washes, front door washes, offerings, paper dyes, and bath teas. And as an herbal mist to effectively cleanse your space.

Draw a symbol in the air over your kettle to quicken the boiling process. Choose herbs that align with your intentions, whether physical (for healing) or magical (for various spells). Brew a tea of rosemary and lavender to relieve a headache. The same tea is great for purification rituals, beauty and love spells, and in encouraging a restful sleep.

Chamomile tea soothes a sore throat and sinus congestion while drawing in prosperity and confidence. These are just a few examples. Stir honey in a clockwise fashion for drawing things to you, counterclockwise for eradicating things from your life.

Cooking Utensils

Every Otherworldly kitchen should have an assortment of utensils like large spoons, spatulas, tongs, and ladles. Why purchase a traditional wand when you can use a magical wooden spoon instead? Many small, witch-owned companies are carving witchy images, elemental symbols, and the like into wooden spoons. I have a set of bamboo spoons that are embellished with moons, the four elements, and witchy sayings that I use daily. If you already have a wooden spoon or two, consider learning how to wood-burn or carve symbols into them yourself. But seriously, a plain wooden spoon works major alchemy in the kitchen.

The Chef's Knife

A block of knives is a boon in the Otherworldly kitchen. But throw out that entire block because you only need one knife in your life. Drumroll please…it's the chef's knife. My husband gifted me a chef's knife last Yule. I haven't had to use another knife since. Slice through potatoes, meat, and all manner of herbs like butter. While slicing and dicing, I imagine my knife is an alchemical tool or ritual athame that transforms ingredients from the mundane to the magical.

I don't recommend using a chef's knife for strictly magical use, though. It's too sharp and too expensive to use on anything except food. Use a cheap, old kitchen knife for inscribing candles, cutting twine, trimming herbs, and more. If you can't afford a chef's knife, use what you have. The first spell I ever cast consisted of an old steak knife, a bottle of McCormick's cinnamon, and a red candle from the dollar store. And yes, it manifested. Probably a little too much.

Cookbooks and Herbal Guides

Where would I be without my trusty collection of cookbooks and herbal guides? In the cold depths of Niflheim, that's where. I have an entire shelf in my kitchen dedicated to antique and vintage ancestral cookbooks and modern cuisine cookbooks. My favorites include: The Art of French Cooking by Julia Child, Salt Fat Acid Heat by Samin Nosrat, Celtic Folklore Cooking by Joanne Asala, Outlander Kitchen by Theresa Carle-Sanders, and Great Easy Meals by Food Network. My favorite herbal guides include Cunningham's Encyclopedia of Magical Herbs, Homegrown Herbs by Tammi Hartung, 20,000 Secrets of Tea by Victoria Zak, Incense Oils and Brews by Scott Cunningham, and Rosemary Gladstar's Medicinal Herbs.

Food Processor

Small, cup-sized food processors are an excellent tool for grinding up herbs in a hurry. I use my small food processor to make quick, loose incense blends. It's much faster than grinding it out in the mortar and pestle. Seriously, sometimes you'll be mortaring for days. A food processor is a wonderful alternative to the manual mortar and pestle. I like my larger, mac-daddy food processor for chopping veggies and blending things like hummus, pesto, and chimichurri. KitchenAid makes a functional and affordable food processor with different blades and settings. I don't recommend investing in a large food processor if you don't like to make herb sauces, chip dips, etc. A small one will do just fine for garlic mincing and incense blending.

Sieve

A sieve is an essential kitchen witch tool for a few reasons. One - it strains herbs out of oils, sprays, floor and door washes. Two – it holds beans, veggies and fruits while rinsing. And three – as a sifter it aerates and separates dry ingredients for baking purposes. In American folk magic traditions, sieves filter out bad dreams when placed under the bed of the afflicted. It can also be hung in the kitchen window to promote positive flow of energy.

Bottles and Jars

Witches love their bottles and jars. It's a real addiction for some of us (shhh, not me). But seriously, any time you're about to throw away an old spice bottle, empty olive or spaghetti sauce jar, or wine bottle, keep it for magical purposes instead. Mason jars are great, but not everyone can afford to buy them new. Re-use and repurpose! Bottles and jars work as containers for herbs, roots, mosses, bark, powders, oils, curios, dirt and more. In addition, many spells can be cast utilizing a bottle or jar.

Food Dehydrator

Ten years ago, I bought a food dehydrator for twenty-five dollars. I use it EVERY. SINGLE. SUMMER. While the cheaper dehydrators won't work well on fruits and veggies like a professional one, they are perfect for dehydrating herbs and flowers. Plus, I've found flowers will retain their original color when put in a food dehydrator, as opposed to air-drying them. If you grow your own herbs and flowers, or forage for wild plants, a food dehydrator is your best friend. And magical bonus points: it makes your house smell amazing. Every Summer my husband's like, "this house smells like an herb garden". That's all because of my food dehydrator. Well, mostly.

Herb Scissors

Another kitchen tool that's helpful for herb gardening is herb scissors. This is a pair of scissors with multiple blades that shreds herbs into tiny bits. Afterwards, you can store your herbs in a jar or bottle. Sure, you could crumble or rip herbs with your hands, but that seems to take forever in my experience. And it doesn't give you even-cut shreds or pieces like herb scissors do. I promise, if you grow your own herbs, get yourself a pair of herb scissors.

Mortar and Pestle

An ancient and traditional tool, the mortar and pestle crushes and grinds down herbs, salts, nuts, and other ingredients into a blend or powder. I've also made red brick dust AND cascarilla powder using a marble mortar and pestle. A modern substitution is the food processor; however, the mortar and pestle are best for releasing oils from fresh herbs, rather than chopping them in a food processor. I have also found the actual process of blending and crushing herb matter by hand is melodic and activates your ingredients. And when your ingredients are charged with intention, your spells yield stronger results.

Coffee Maker

Your coffee maker is a magical, Otherworldly apparatus. Press a button and beguiling bean juice spews forth, bringing us back from the dead every single morning. If you didn't guess, coffee has many magical uses. Adding coffee or coffee beans to a spell will speed it up and boost the energy ten-fold. In addition, adding a cup of black coffee to a bath purifies the aura and wards off negative entities. Not to mention, who doesn't love the smell of coffee in the morning? The aroma itself is supernatural. Coffee serves as an offering for ancestors. I know my grandad loved his coffee every morning, so I brew him a cup often. Coffee makes a natural dye for grimoire pages, wooden tools, and fabric.

Cast Iron Skillet

    Our cast iron skillet debuts on the weekends when we make big family breakfasts. Cooking with it aligns with family love and joyfully reminds me that it's the weekend. To relax and enjoy your time together. Cast iron in the Otherworldly kitchen wards off trickster spirits and negative energy. The best thing about cast iron is you can use it on the stove, put it in the oven and over an open fire. It's durable and magical on so many levels. If you've let your cast iron build up a hard residue, save the scrapings and add them to your next batch of witch's black salt.

Chopping Boards

    A practical tool no one can do without is the chopping board. I have multiple chopping boards. I find that I like the plastic kind the best for everyday use. I know some folks will say never use plastic, but the issue with using wood to chop meats is that the wood will collect bacteria. Whereas the plastic is less likely to hold onto microbes and can be sterilized in extremely hot water. I typically reserve my wooden boards for chopping veggies, fruits, and herbs. And I save the plastic board for meats.

    The wooden chopping boards are pretty. You can have a special chopping board carved with your family's surname. OR here's another fun idea – have runes, magical symbols, or even your intentions burned or carved into the chopping board to make it super powerful. There are woodworkers on Etsy who specialize in this type of work. Chopping boards are necessary for protecting your counters when slicing and dicing veggies, meats, herbs, fruits, and for cutting pizzas. Wooden chopping boards are also fun displays for charcuterie spreads on sabbats and esbats.

Kitchen Witch Guardian Dolls

What is a kitchen guardian spirit? A kitchen guardian spirit is a familiar spirit specially tasked with aiding your magickal kitchen workings. Its other important duty is to watch over the household and prevent your family from meeting harmful spirits, energies, and illness. Here is my personal spell to summon your own kitchen guardian spirit and how to house it in a kitchen witch doll or vessel. If you can find a kitchen witch doll online, purchase one that calls to you. If you can make one, all the better. But if you don't like the idea of a doll, a vessel such as a jar, vase, or bottle works well too.

What You'll Need:

- a poppet, doll, statue, or vessel to house your kitchen guardian spirit (I purchased a vintage kitchen witch statue from Etsy to house my kitchen spirit, but you can make or buy a doll, or use a bottle or jar. What you need is a vessel to be the spirit's home within your home)
- a white 7-day candle (or small-medium white pillar)
- a handful of wormwood (substitute with Mugwort, catnip, OR a combination of lavender and sandalwood)
- a bit of loose-leaf tobacco
- olive oil
- a chopstick or thick needle

How to Summon a Kitchen Guardian Spirit:

1. This summoning spell is best performed on the Full Moon when spirits are most active, and manifestation is at its most powerful.
2. Go to your kitchen. Cleanse the space thoroughly in whatever way you prefer. Also cleanse your candle and doll/vessel.
3. Next get into a relaxed alpha state of mind with music, chanting, incense, etc.
4. Take your chopstick or thick needle and poke 3 holes into the candle about 2-3 inches deep.
5. Sprinkle the wormwood into each hole while stating "wormwood draw to me, the familiar spirit that's good and right for me, to protect my house and family, and guard my hearth wholly." Say this at least 3, 7, 9, or 13 times. If you feel drawn to chant or sing the incantation, go for it.
6. Now light the candle and place it on the stove next to your doll/vessel.
7. Next, offer the tobacco to the familiar spirit. You can light it as incense on a charcoal, if you'd like, or sprinkle it around the doll/vessel. And say, "tobacco draw my kitchen guardian spirit to me, benevolent familiar spirit, hear me. I give you this offering gratefully."
8. Take a bit of olive oil, rub it on your hands, then dress the doll with the oil. Start from the bottom and rub up until you've covered the entire doll/vessel from bottom to top. While doing this chant, "kitchen guardian take heart. You have a safe place at this hearth. May this doll/vessel I've prepared be your home. May we benefit each other until your spirit must roam." Repeat 3, 7, 9 or 13 times. Again, chanting and singing is welcome.

9. After you've invited the familiar spirit in, let the candle burn for at least an hour and keep it beside the doll/vessel on the stove. The candleflame acts as a beacon to draw the right familiar spirit to your kitchen.
10. Once you've extinguished the candle, you must set your kitchen guardian spirit's doll/vessel somewhere it won't be handled by others. Keep the candle in your kitchen and light it once a day for 7 days next to your kitchen guardian spirit's doll/vessel.
11. You'll need to name your kitchen guardian but don't let anyone outside your household know its name. Talk to your kitchen spirit every day and provide regular offerings.

More Kitchen Witch Tools and Ingredients

Truly, what you feel is necessary to shift the vibe in your kitchen and give you the tools you need to make magic is entirely up to you. But there are a few more things I recommend: hanging a string of peppers or garlic bulbs in your kitchen to ward off negativity, keeping an array of candles handy, and a decent stock of incense. I also keep a variety of pots and pans of all sizes, colanders, containers, a knife sharpener, and much more.

Chapter 6

The Lucky Living Room

Next, we come to the Living Room, also called the Family Room. It's the area where everyone tends to gather, second only to the kitchen. After a long day, what do we do but come home, kick off our shoes, and collapse on the couch? The living room is our special place to relax, recuperate, and connect with family members or housemates. In centuries past, the living area was all part of the same room, with the hearth centrally located. The kitchen and living area were once the same space. Which I find particularly interesting, because today, everyone wants an "open concept". This is a kitchen and living room in one big room with no separating walls. We are going back in time a bit with this "open floor" concept, aren't we? No matter how your living room is set up, you can make it the Otherworldly living room of your dreams.

The living room is linked to the earth element. It's a place where we feel grounded and cozy. Loved and whole. Like being wrapped up in Mother Earth's warm embrace. Naturally, we tend to add decorations and pieces to this space that are rooted in the earth element: wooden end tables, coffee tables, houseplants, and pictures of loved ones. Even ottomans and recliners where we kick up our feet are connected to the earth (think metal, wood, and a second place to put our feet besides the ground).

When creating your Otherworldly living room, the first thing to consider is whether you and your family find it comfortable. I know this seems obvious, but if the space doesn't feel warm and inviting to you, it doesn't feel warm and inviting to others. Remedy this in an affordable way by adding more throw pillows and blankets. Rearrange the furniture in a way that allows for entertainment and personal connection. For example, in my living room, we have the couch and ottoman facing the TV. In the opposite corners, we have reclining chairs that face the couch. When we host family and friends, this set-up gives everyone a place to sit and positions us in a way that encourages people to talk and connect.

The Ancestral Altar

An appropriate place for an ancestral altar, the living room allows for all members of the family to feel the presence of their ancestors. Of course, working with ancestors isn't for everyone, so if you don't feel drawn to do it, don't. But if you do, set up your ancestral altar in the living room. This allows your ancestors to see the daily goings-on of your family. This simple act makes the ancestors feel as if they're a living, breathing part of the family. From their sacred spot in the living room, they will protect and guide you and your family.

If you've never built an ancestral altar before, how do you do it? It's not as difficult or as expensive as it seems. First, decide on a surface. If you have a fireplace, the mantle is the absolute perfect place, as it links you to the ancestral hearths of the past. The blazing hearth fire in your home is the same fire that kept your ancestors warm, fed, and alive.

If you don't have a fireplace in your living room, choose a spot that won't be used for anything else. For example, a hutch or credenza, a bookshelf, or even a shelf inside of a glass cabinet. Your ancestral altar is a holy place meant only for the ancestors' energy. Which means it's *not* the place for remotes, keys, gaming consoles, phones, plates, coasters, toys, or anything that doesn't represent or is specifically consecrated for ancestral work. It's just about being respectful. I've had people set their keys, purses, and phones down on my ancestral altars before. What do I do? Have a mini panic attack inside, then wait for them to leave and cleanse the altar ferociously. This might not be your reaction, but I'm just keeping it real.

Once you've decided on the location, putting your altar together is simple. Start with a representation of your ancestors: pictures, heirlooms, and mementos. I've had people ask me, is it okay to put pictures of living family members on the altar? It truly depends on what you believe. Some traditions warn against it because it may make certain ancestors jealous of the living. I've always kept the living separate from the dead on my altars. But again, the choice is yours.

Heirlooms passed down through the family bring grounding energy to your altar. And they act as a tangible energy channel between your ancestors and the altar space. Heirlooms are those precious pieces that have been handed down in your family. Things like your great grandmother's string of pearls, your grandfather's police badge, a great aunt's handkerchief, basically anything that was once an ancestor's. You can include a printed map of your ancestral homeland. Small statues of animals linked to your family. Is your family named after an animal? Have you looked up your family's Coat of Arms? Images of these animals and plants are great additions to the ancestral altar.

Once your ancestors are represented on the altar, add offering bowls and cups. Maybe you have a porcelain bowl that your grandmother gave you. Or a silver tray. Additionally, candles and candle holders, incense and incense burners, and divination tools for ancestral communication are welcome and useful. I've also used linen, doilies, and embroidered tablecloths made by my ancestors as altar cloths.

Seasonal décor is festive and appropriate on the ancestral altar. For example, a small Yule log, Yule goat, evergreen garland, and suns for Yuletide. Eggs, birds' nests, and pastel colors for the Spring Equinox. Floral wreaths, mini maypoles, and fairy figurines for Midsummer. Use your intuition and imagination to build your sacred ancestral space. As you continue to work with your ancestors and use your altar more and more, it will grow and evolve. And take on a life of itself. You'll be able to simply stand in front of it and feel your ancestors' energy radiating off it.

I enjoy giving my ancestors regular offerings to show my appreciation. This includes a cup of water that I refresh daily, candlelight and prayer weekly, and other items like letters of appreciation, coins, stones, poetry, and jewelry. What you give to your ancestors should be driven by your intuition and by what you can afford. Don't worry. Your ancestors will tell you what they like and dislike. They also appreciate alcohol, tobacco, herbs, flowers, and the occasional lavish meal. If you leave food or beverage for your ancestors, remove the remnants in a timely fashion. Don't let anything mold over, rot, or start to stink on your altar. That's a sign of disrespect, and the last time I checked, the ancestors are all about r-e-s-p-e-c-t.

Charms for Peace and Harmony

Maybe it's just me, but I feel like the mood in the living room spreads to the rest of the house. Which means the best place to promote peace and harmony in the home is the living room. You can cast spells for this intention, or you can purposely enchant items and place them in your living room to keep the positive vibes flowing. I'll give you a few suggestions.

Place black tourmaline next to your Television, gaming console, and other electronics in your living room. This powerful stone absorbs electromagnetic waves from technology, essentially blocking negative energy before it makes it to you. A Himalayan pink salt lamp is helpful in removing negative ions from the air and replacing them with soothing, loving vibes. And, of course, rose quartz goes well in the living room, just like it does in literally every other room.

Shift the energy in your living room from plain to Otherworldly by adding candlelight and incense. I prefer scented candles for this purpose, like linen, vanilla, lavender, and teakwood. But you can use any candles you choose. Sometimes folks can't use candles because of house rules or allergies. In this case, LED battery-powered candles are just fine! I've seen witches online scold others for using LED candles…that they aren't "real fire", so they don't have the same effect. I don't know if it will have the same effect when it comes to spells, but what I do know is this. Batteries provide power to those candles. Therefore, there is a flow of energy. Therefore, that battery-powered energy can shift a room's vibes too. I have used LED candles on my ancestral altar which is housed inside my wooden wardrobe. Obviously using real candles in a wooden wardrobe is a bad idea. So, LED candles it is.

The same goes with incense. Some people can't use incense due to health reasons or rules. Some people live in dorms or share a space with others who don't like the smell of incense. That's perfectly all right. You can substitute with an essential oil diffuser. Diffusers are affordable and typically don't irritate people's allergies as greatly as smoke. Diffusing essential oils in the living room shifts the vibe via the practice of aromatherapy. My recommendations are lavender to promote peace and beauty, jasmine to increase love, and orange to brighten dull spirits. But there are hundreds of essential oils on the market. Just be careful which ones you diffuse, as some can be harmful to animals, babies, etc. Do your research if you're unsure.

      My recommendations above are all discreet ways of turning your living space into an Otherworldly oasis. If you live with people who aren't privy to your magical self, they might not notice one way or another. In addition, houseplants serve as living spells to aid your intentions. If you have a bright, cheery living room, you have lots of options for houseplants. Infuse your spell intentions into a houseplant by writing your intentions on a piece of paper and burying it in the plant's soil. Feed your houseplants with moon water to add an extra layer of serenity to your Otherworldly living room. Or sun water to give new life to a dying plant.

Chapter 7

The Beguiled Bathroom

We have come a long way from the days of outhouses and chamber pots, haven't we? Today, most of us have a bathroom or washroom, which conveniently houses a toilet, a bathtub and/or shower, a sink and vanity with a mirror. We are *so* spoiled. In the past, our ancestors were visiting the woods or streets, outhouses, or relieving themselves in chamber pots and then dumping it out the window. YES, that happened and in some places it still does. If you find yourself with a functioning bathroom, you are lucky indeed. So why not appreciate it and magically enhance this space and the overall experience? That's right. I want you to feel magical in the shower, bathtub, at the sink AND on the john.

As for bathing, our ancestors often didn't bathe except once a month, sometimes even less. It was dependent on access to a water source and if the weather permitted it. Think about it. You wouldn't take daily baths if you lived in a harsh, cold place in the North like Finland or Iceland. Have you ever heard the phrase, "don't throw the baby out with the bath water?" We can trace this strange saying to a time when people shared the bath water. The father would typically take his bath first, then the mother, then the older children on down the line to the youngest. Most people didn't have running water and had to source their bath water from a nearby lake, river, or creek. Or they had wells, which might be dried up. Or they lived in a place and time when water had to be conserved.

The same goes for the running water that fills our sinks. Before sinks, our ancestors sourced their water from a spring, or pumped well water into a trough or basin. More recently, our ancestors might have had a pitcher and basin they'd use for "washing up". This is what you'd use to wash your face and hands before a meal. You might have seen something like it in the series Anne with an E or Bridgerton. Today, we are blessed to have a faucet with running water and a sink with a drain. Oh, and the drain? It automatically sucks the dirty water out of sight. Modern magic, indeed.

How do we make our bathroom an enchanted place? Can it be a place for spells, ritual, and everyday magic? Every space in the Otherworldly Household is magical when sanctified and treated with respect and love. First, keep your bathroom as clean as you can. Don't let months roll by before cleaning your tub. Don't let the toothpaste globs pile high as a mountain in the sink. I try to clean my bathroom at least once a week – the *entire* thing. But, if you're physically unable to clean to this level on a weekly basis, do little things to keep your bathroom in tip top shape. Run a rag over the vanity to remove dust and debris and brush the toilet bowl if that's all you can do. If your bathroom has a window, open it to shake up the energy and remove lingering, funky air.

Magical Bathroom Decorations

Now it's time to decorate. The great thing about the bathroom is it's typically small, so you don't have to spend a ton of money embellishing it. Think about whether you'd like to incorporate a witchy theme. Fun themes for the Otherworldly bathroom should focus on the water element: beach scenes, seashells, bottles of sand, and sea glass. Sea creatures like turtles, dolphins, whales, and sea birds add a whimsical touch. Although, I don't recommend over-doing the sea life theme. It tends to look a little cheesy.

In addition, this is one of the rooms in your house you can get away with a mermaid theme. One of my family members has a beautiful painting of a mermaid sleeping on a beach. She put it into a golden frame and hung it in the bathroom. I've always admired this fairy-tale piece, and it even inspired me to find my own mermaid art for my bathroom.

You can find affordable, magical accoutrements at second-hand stores, flea markets, and garage sales. Dollar stores carry glass bottles and jars to fill with seashells, sand, sea glass, seagull feathers and other miscellaneous beachcombed treasures. Collect and add Otherworldly pieces to your bathroom over time. I've said it once. And I'll say it again. You don't have to do a complete overhaul of your home. Take it little by little. Put a candle on each of your bathroom vanities, in front of the mirrors. Add faux (or real) houseplants on the back of the toilet or in the bathroom window. Plants are decorative and naturally cleanse the air. Plus, if you choose a succulent for the bathroom, it will naturally acquire some of its water from the air (think of how steamy your bathroom is while the shower is running).

If you have the space on an empty wall, a small shrine or altar honoring a water deity or spirit brings in that liminal energy. My only recommendation is you don't put an altar on the back of the toilet OR have the altar directly facing the toilet. Most gods don't want to see you or your family members and guests relieving themselves. Though I have heard that some Djinn relish bathrooms as their hang-out spot. And I recently learned of a Toilet God in the Chinese pantheon. So, who knows? Again, how you set your bathroom altars up is your call.

Water Gods and Goddesses

I'd like to introduce you to a few sea gods and goddesses who may find your washroom a comfortable spot to visit. Whomever you choose to work with in your practice is up to you. I won't tell you that you must be of that god's culture. You know in your heart what is right for you and your personal spiritual path. I am listing deities from various pantheons to be as inclusive as I can without overstepping my boundaries. If you don't vibe with these gods, a simple Google search will yield a whole mess of results on "sea gods". The point here is to always do your research and be respectful of ALL deities and cultures.

Atargatis

An ancient Syrian goddess, Atargatis reminds me of Aphrodite. In fact, her cult could very well have influenced Aphrodite's. Atargatis is typically depicted as a half-woman half-fish creature (yes, think mermaid) and her sacred animals are fish and doves. She is a protector of women, children, fertility, and water. Sounds awfully familiar.

Aphrodite

Aphrodite is arguably the most famous goddess in the world. She is an ancient Greek goddess, however she likely originated in ancient Mesopotamia. Scholars believe her name means "risen from the sea" or "bright". Depending on the myth, Aphrodite has no parents or was born of Ouranus' semen, when his genitals were cast into the sea. His semen created seafoam and hence Aphrodite was born of the sea *and* sky. She is mostly known for being a deity who rules over romantic love. Maintain an altar for her with items that represent water like seashells and sand, as well as items that represent love like sexual images and hearts. Offer her perfume, incense, wine, and fresh water.

Cliodhna

An obscure ancient Celtic goddess, Cliodhna (pronounced Klee-nah) was once an ancestral deity of the people of Munster, a province in Ireland. She is a beautiful goddess who lives in a glass castle in the Celtic Otherworld, where her magical birds sing songs of renewal and healing. Over time, and as the pagans converted to Christianity, she became a siren, faery, Queen of the Banshees and then lastly an evil, child-snatching hag. But if we back up, we can see her link to the water clearly. In the old faery tales, she lives on a magical island across the sea. So, it makes sense in later folklore that she would become a mermaid or a siren.

Khnum

The ancient Egyptians had no shortage of deities linked to the water element. Why? Because their lives depended on the Nile River for survival. The Nile fed their crops, provided a water source, and acted as a means of transportation for trade between Lower and Upper Egypt. If the Nile over-flooded, it destroyed people's homes. If it didn't flood enough, crops struggled, and the people went hungry. The gods played an important part in the balance of the floods every year. One of the deities that ruled over the Nile floods is Khnum. Khnum is a ram-headed god who ruled over the waters, as well as a creator god who was credited with the creation of man.

Poseidon

Another well-known deity originating in Greece is the sea god Poseidon. He was one of the twelve mighty Olympians in Greek myth and presided over the sea, storms, horses, and earthquakes. You have likely seen an image of him on the TV, in movies, or even read about him as a fictional character in modern literature. When he manifests, his face is seen in seafoam or in breaking waves. He's also been known to ride his horses over the ocean, creating large waves in his wake. His ancient Roman counterpart is Neptune.

The Tub and Shower

I've mentioned the importance of keeping your Otherworldly Household clean. Well, I won't lecture you about it again, but suffice to say, if you plan to use your tub or shower in bathing rituals, cleanliness is crucial. Truly, the bathtub and shower are some of the most magical spaces in the entire house. Once again, we have a direct source of water at our fingertips.

Many spells and rituals can be done in the bathtub. Obviously cleansing rituals are a popular choice, but you can cast spells for nearly any intention in your tub or shower. Some of my most powerful ritual baths weren't even for cleansing, but for initiation, vitality, renewal, and rebirth. These were beautiful pagan baptisms in which I'd submerge myself in the water, symbolically entering the Otherworld, then emerging a new and changed witch. Baths and showers are a compelling way to break runs of bad luck, hexes, jinxes, and curses. Cord cutting rituals can even be performed while in the tub. Simply lay back and close your eyes. Then envision or feel for the energetic cords that may be attached to your aura. Use your hands like scissors and sever the ties that bind. Then dip under the water completely to remove any lingering negative residue. You'll step out of the bath feeling amazing!

Some witches make the mistake of mimicking the elaborate baths they see online. And then they end up spending way too much energy cleaning up the remnants. You know those pretty pictures of bathtubs filled with flower petals, sparkles, floating candles, and the like? These baths are beautiful but not practical. Have you ever tried cleaning plant matter out of the bottom of your tub? It not only takes a long time, but it also clogs your drain.

    Instead, add your herbs, flowers, and salts to a muslin bag or sachet then throw it into the hot water when you're ready. You can also put a small metal shower strainer over your drain. This will act as a colander to catch the herb material as the water drains out. These methods save your back and cut down on minutes of work. OR you could craft a bath tea. Infuse herbs in at least sixteen ounces of simmering water and allow the mixture to cool slightly. Then pour your magical bath tea into the hot water in your tub. I promise all three of these methods are just as effective and much more practical than the popular online witch aesthetic.

    Shower stalls are just as magical as bathtubs. You have an automatic waterfall at your disposal. When showering, visualize standing under a beautiful waterfall allowing the water to cascade down on top of you. Bathing you in white light and loving energy. You can put on music or even waterfall sounds while you're in the shower to add to the cleansing effect. Hang a sachet of herbs over your shower head to allow the water to flow through the herbs then onto you. There's even something called a "shower tab" on the market. It's made of salts, oils, and herbs. When a hot shower steams up, the tab slowly dissolves, releasing its aromas in the air all around you. These can be used in alignment with your intentions: lavender to relax, peppermint to purify, orange to energize, chamomile to relieve sinus congestion, etc.

The Toilet

    You might be wondering why I'm including the toilet in the Otherworldly Household's magical appliances. It does seem a bit off-putting, I'll admit. But don't exclude the power of the louvre when it comes to banishing spells. Have a toxic habit you're trying to quit? An ex of whom you can't seem to get out of your head? Write that habit or toxic relationship on a piece of toilet paper and FLUSH it, baby! Other than that, I have no further recommendations on toilet rituals. Unless, of course, you're working with the Toilet God. In which case, there may be other ways to use the toilet in your rituals.

The Bathroom Mirror

Second to running water, the mirror is the most magical tool in the bathroom. Coincidentally, mirrors are connected to the water element. Think about it. The first mirror ever used was a reflecting pool. An early, primal ancestor peered into a calm body of water and saw her image reflected at her. Following this discovery, mirrors were made from reflective stone like obsidian, then later from metal and finally glass.

Your bathroom mirror is a portal. A door. A tool to gaze at the other side and so much more. It's just as effective as any other magical mirror for beauty, self-love, and self-confidence spells. When I'm feeling down about myself, I'll write a few self-love affirmations on a post-it note and slap it on the bathroom mirror. I've even written self-love notes using lipstick or eyeliner (side note, if you don't use eyeliner and are laughing at me right now, keep in mind I'm from a generation who adored their black liquid liner!)

Beyond mirror love notes, this amazing tool is successful in spells for finding one's true self, performing past life regressions, and contacting spirits beyond the veil. One warning with using mirrors to contacts spirits – make sure you know how to lock the portal when you're done. I believe mirrors allow us to see into other dimensions and planes of existence. But I also believe they can act as doorways for spirits who are strong enough to push through them into our reality. Keep that in mind. Personally, for scrying, spirit contact and reversals, I use a small, hand-held mirror that isn't plastered to the wall. This way I can handle the mirror easily, as well as conceal it when I'm finished with my working. But again, the choice is yours.

If you've inherited a mirror that is showing signs of spirit activity, first try cleansing it with water *and* smoke. Then draw a protective rune or symbol on it to magically lock it. I've also known witches to hang a bag of salt or witch's bells over a particularly powerful or chaotic mirror. Keep in mind, when two mirrors face each other, this is an easy way for spirits to use your home as a pathway between dimensions. Spirits will jump between realms using mirrors. It's a mirror matrix, folks. So, maybe keep your mirrors facing away from each other, if possible.

Chapter 8

The Bewitched Bedroom

We can relax, let down our guard, and just be ourselves in our bedrooms. The bedroom is a place of healing, contemplation, preparation, and lovemaking. Not only do we spend seven or more hours sleeping in this room, we spend another hour or more getting ourselves ready for the day, reading a book at the end of the night, or spending quality romantic time with our partners. When we are sick or in pain, we curl up in bed with our blankets, pillows, and furry friends. What a sacred space in the Otherworldly Household!

Once again, we are so lucky to be living today. I know there's a lot of things wrong with the world, but there are a lot of things right too. Our ancestors may have shared their bed with the entire family. Sometimes the bed was in a loft area, separate from the hearth and living space. Sometimes the bed was in the same room as the kitchen and living space. For some folks, it's still like this. What's most important is that we have a roof over our heads and loving people around us. And if you're blessed with a private, cozy bedroom, take advantage of its magic and blessings.

First, is your bedroom as cozy as you'd like it to be? If not, how can you make it so? Add more pillows, warm, soft blankets, and new sheets to the bed. A set of fifteen-hundred thread count Egyptian cotton sheets aren't required, but how about t-shirt sheets from Walmart for forty bucks? If you can't afford new sheets, don't worry about it. Rearranging your bedroom furniture can convert the space into an inviting witch's burrow. Not to mention, rearranging your furniture shakes up old, stale energy. And flowing energy in the bedroom = more romance = happy partner and (more importantly) a happier you.

Turn on the fan to keep the air moving in the bedroom. Fiery passion in the bedroom needs a little air to keep it burning. And what about curtains? Do you work a night shift and sleep during the day? Or maybe you enjoy sleeping in on the weekends? Grab yourself a heavy set of blackout curtains to shield the sun during those much-needed moments of sleep. Sleep is so important for your health and for your magical practice. In this state, we are open to messages from the other side. It's also often when our astral bodies leave our physical bodies and travel to other dimensions. Plus, if you're not getting enough sleep, you won't have the energy to cast spells or perform ritual.

The bedroom is linked to two elements: fire and water. The fire element erupts in the bedroom between romantic partners with love and sex. The water flows in with emotions, sleep, and dream time. Magic in the bedroom comes in many forms including sex magic, love and self-love spells, dream work, intuition, psychic abilities, journaling, spells for peace and comfort, healing energy work and astral travel.

Magical Bedroom Decorations

How you decorate your bedroom depends on your style and preferences. Acquire paintings of gods and goddesses, people making love, faery scenes, and other magical themes in bed and bath stores, department stores, art galleries, second-hand stores, and on websites like eBay and Etsy. Decorate with items that call to you and evoke the fiery and watery elements of the Otherworldly bedroom.

Other charmed boudoir items might take the form of a Himalayan salt lamp (I know I've mentioned them before, but there's a reason, okay?), crystals and crystal towers, and sexy photos of you and your partner. Some witches hang dream catchers over the bed to filter out bad dreams. If you choose to, keep in mind, genuine dream catchers should be purchased from specific indigenous tribes of North America. And the energy from "snagged dreams" will build up in the dream catcher, so cleanse it every once in a blue moon.

The Bed

Bow chicka wow wow. The key feature in the bedroom is the bed. What magic can be accomplished with a bed? The obvious things include sex magic (with your partner or yourself), love magic, and dream work. But what about protecting yourself during sleep? Can we enchant our beds with protective spells and positive energy? Absolutely!

Cast spells over the bed and the perimeter: hang charms above the bed, off the bed posts, headboard, and footboards, under the mattress or place items directly under the bed. You have a lot of options here. You can also put charms in your pillowcases, under your pillow, or on the nightstand.

Here are some ideas for potent bed charms:

- Spell bags: fill muslin bags and sachets with herbs, stones, and other trinkets and placed under the mattress, hung from bed posts, and placed under the pillow to induce dreams, astral travel, attract love and promote healing.
- Spell bags can also be made specifically to protect the sleeping individual from psychic attack.

- Charge an amulet with protective energy and hang above the bed.
- Place a broom under the bed for protection during dream time. Use this same method in sympathetic magic for "flying" to the witch's sabbat.
- Hang a willow branch above the bed to guard from psychic attack and lightning strikes.
- Put iron under the crib to shield a child from being carried away by the faeries.
- A bowl of salt under the bed absorbs negative energy and protects from evil spirits while asleep.
- If you're being attacked in your sleep, place a cup or bowl of water under the bed to soak up negative energy and reduce nightmares.
- Place a piece of red string under the pillow to ensure a safe return from the Otherworld at night. The red string represents the umbilical cord that connects your astral body and your physical body. AND it symbolizes our ancestral bloodline.

The Dresser Drawers

Our dressers and dressing tables have the important job of holding our clothing and other personal items. It keeps our garments clean, private, and safe. We can also utilize dressers to conceal certain spells and charms. For instance, if you've cast a candle spell for love, bag up the remnants and stuff it in your underwear drawer. If you've cast a travel spell to attain the vacation of your dreams, keep the spell remnants in your sock drawer (or in a shoe). Your creativity will take flight when seeing your furniture and other household items through the eyes of an astute witch. Which is just the witch that you are!

Another fun way to add a magical element to your dresser is by setting crystals, candles, and deity statues on top. I also bury sachets of sweet-smelling flowers like lavender and rosebuds in my dresser drawers. Every time I open the drawer, a lovely floral aroma wafts out, PLUS it scents the clothing next to it.

The Closet and Wardrobe

I'm lucky. I have an antique wardrobe given to me by my grandmother, and I have a large closet in my bedroom. Wardrobes, armoires, and closets are akin to the dresser in that they magically *protect* and *conceal*. And they physically aid us in organization. So, when wondering what kind of witchcraft can be done in the closet or armoire, think hiding and protecting.

We can also view the closet and wardrobe as liminal spaces. A place that's in-between – it's not quite its own room but it's not part of the bedroom exactly either. Don't believe it's liminal? Have you read The Lion, The Witch and the Wardrobe? The Wardrobe in this classic book is a doorway to another world…a magical world called Narnia with witches and fantastical creatures. Turn the key to your wardrobe, open the door, and you just might meet a talking fox, mischievous faun, or Wintry Empress. But a quick warning here – don't eat the Turkish delight!

But a wardrobe isn't required to harness the energy of a liminal space. The closet is the same concept. Whether it's walk-in or not. If you need to conceal a spell from others, the closet or wardrobe is the perfect place to keep it. The wardrobe acts as a witch's cabinet, if not needed for other mundane purposes. I have turned my antique wardrobe into a witchy cabinet. I preserve a large array of occult books, Tarot and oracle decks, runes and charm bags, wands, and ritual robes inside. And, because it's equipped with wooden shelves, I've turned the left half into a large shrine for my gods, goddesses, ancestors, and animal allies. I see the wardrobe as a door to the spirit world. When I open it, I'm opening the line of communication between me and my guides. When I place a spell or charm inside, I'm placing it in that liminal space to be charged by the Otherworld.

Chapter 9

The "Other" Rooms

We've covered the main room that make up the Otherworldly Household, but we haven't quite covered *every* room. Every home is built differently and will have variations in how rooms are structurally designed, where closets are situated, as well as pantries, crawlspaces, hallways, entryways, patios and more. Many of these "other" spaces serve as a precipice between you and the spirit world. And you can employ them as such.

The attic is a liminal space - it's not quite a living area but it's not outside either. It's *within* the house but not the *main* part of the house. It's the space between us and the heavens…between us and the gods. Turn your attic into an enchanted chamber where you cast spells, talk to spirits, and meet with deity. In the Victorian era, it was common practice to have seances in the attic. I'll bet this is because attics are creepy, but I also think it's ingrained in us to call on spirits in spaces like the attic. I suspect spirits occasionally get trapped in the attic on their way out. Thus, making it easier for us to contact them. This is why witches open the windows when a family member is dying. To allow the spirit to leave the home with ease.

Think of the cellar or basement as a similar concept to the attic. Except, this space isn't between us and the gods, it's between us and the dead. In Old Norse belief, the realm of the dead was underneath us. Somewhere deep inside the roots of Yggdrasil (the World Tree) …deep within the earth. The idea of an Underworld isn't an exception to the Norse religion, but to many ancient peoples. The Celts believed the Tuatha de Danann (a godly race of faery people) dwelled in the earth and could access our world through faery mounds. They also believed the dead sometimes went to a place located under the ocean floor. Even if you ask a Christian, where is Hell? He instinctively points downward. Therefore, spirit communication is incredibly powerful when conducted in a basement, nestled inside the first layer of Mother Earth.

Other rooms that are neither here nor there include hallways, crawlspaces, cupboards under the stairs, balconies, patios, and porches. If your home has any of these special spaces, use them to your advantage. The hallways in my home are large and spacious enough to house things like altars and witchy cabinets. But, if you have a small hallway, hang photos of your ancestors or spirit guides on the walls. When I was growing up, my grandmother had a mirror hanging at the far end of the hallway. Isn't it odd that I was always terrified of what I'd see in that ornate golden mirror? Hallways are a space that attract spirits…it's a passageway for us AND for them. This is why you'll notice more movement out of the corners of your eyes in the hallways at night than anywhere else in the house. If these shadows freak you out, just shut your bedroom door. Easily solved. Or refer to the section on how to protect your household from unwanted spirits.

Bewitch these "other" rooms. Add altars and invoke deities you feel fit those spaces. Altars can be constructed anywhere in the Otherworldly Household. Break out your Tarot cards and pendulum in the rooms where you feel a jolt of energy. Just be prepared to talk to the spirits there – the spirit of your house, ancestors, guides, elementals and more. They will guide you further.

Chapter 10

The Sacred Garden

When you're not inside your Otherworldly Household, where might you be on your property? Are you hanging out in the backyard or strolling through the garden? Are you sitting on your balcony, watching the sun rise or set? My most magical experiences in nature have happened on the property surrounding my house. You don't have to go far to achieve alignment with the Earth. Simply walk out your front door.

Whether you have a full-fledged backyard with a garden, it doesn't truly matter. Even if you live in an apartment building with no land to call your own, there are ways to connect with the Earth. Take a walk. Get your feet on the same ground that supports your house's foundation. If the weather is nice, take your shoes off and walk through the grass. Sit under a tree and read a witchy book. Research and work with the trees, plants, animals, and insects living around your home. My most powerful spells have included ingredients foraged in my own backyard and neighborhood. A feather, a pinecone, a wildflower, a handful of dirt, a magnolia seed, a whisper in the wind.

If you've been thinking of starting a garden, now's your chance. Start small with two herb plants. And work your way up to the fussier fruit trees and vegetables. I've found if you do your research and grow local *native* plants, you'll have a much easier time keeping the plants alive. Even if you have a brown thumb, your area's native plants will thrive under your care. Trust me. In addition, growing native plants means you'll provide shelter or a food source for pollinators like butterflies, moths, birds, bees and even bats. Once you start growing your garden, you'll be utterly amazed that it becomes its own little eco-system supporting the greater eco-system.

Making magic in your backyard or garden is a simple feat. Especially if you have privacy from nosy neighbors. If you don't, it's easy to be discreet with your outside spell-work. Wait until the day-walkers are in bed for the night. Or disguise your spell-work as benign gardening chores. Need to bury a spell jar? Well, you also need to remove that dead plant at the back of the garden. Do both at the same time. Leaving offerings for the garden faeries might be as straightforward as filling a bird feeder in the Winter. Or cleaning and filling a bird bath. Offerings to local wildlife serve as offerings to land spirits.

Some witches are lucky enough to have property to design an entire garden to meet their ritual needs. If this is you, go for it! Design your garden in spiral shapes, circles, and separate sections of herbs into a Wheel of the Year. If this isn't you, and space is limited, opt for potted plants on the back porch. Don't have a porch? Use your balcony or a sunny window instead. I know witches who have grow-lights in closets, chock-full of rosemary, parsley, dill, chamomile, and whatever magical herbs their witchy hearts desire.

Attracting Fae to the Otherworldly Garden

"Most faeries hate profuse displays of thanks from humans whom they have helped. It is best not to utter thanks at all, but to leave out extra portions of milk, butter, or bread for them by way of showing your appreciation. These offerings are called libations…" (McCoy, 2002)

Milk and Dairy Offerings for the Faeries

The custom of leaving libations for faeries dates back centuries. Milk farmers in Ireland would leave out a libation after every milking to keep the faeries happy. A fed, happy faery was less likely to cause trouble on the farm. Libations of mead or bowls of barley were also common faery offerings. Faeries are finicky and don't like to be thanked or doted over, so quietly leave your faery offerings in the garden.

Faery Food and Libations:
Traditionally, faeries loved sweets, so anything you've baked at home is a perfect offering. If you offer fruit, make sure it is organic. If the birds and ants won't eat it, neither will the faeries. They also love traditional offerings like milk, wine, ale, cream, and mead.

- milk
- honey
- mead
- wine
- ale
- bread
- cakes
- fruit
- cookies
- candy
- bannocks
- colcannon

Other Offerings

In addition to food offerings, the faeries appreciate shiny baubles and trinkets. Ever had a necklace go missing then turn up somewhere completely obvious? This was probably a mischievous faery! Sparkly offerings like jewelry, crystals, stones, and sea glass are appropriate. I've also cast a knot spell using purple cord, seashells, bells and feathers to attract the faeries. Faeries like Celtic flute music, tinkly windchimes, and people who care for the earth and wildlife. Make your gardening ventures an offering to the faeries.

What NOT To Do When Working with Faeries
Yes, there are things you can do to attract the faeries to your garden, but there's also things you shouldn't do. Here's a quick rundown:

- Don't hang horseshoes above your door.
- Don't put iron anywhere you want the faeries to visit (the exception here, I've found, is that household faeries don't mind cast iron skillets in the kitchen).
- There shouldn't be any salt sprinkled around your house or in the garden (the exception here is the Slavic hearth spirit the Domovoi, who actually prefers salt as an offering).
- Deep, loud bells aren't preferred because they scare the garden faeries away (it reminds them of church bells to which they are averse).
- No clergymen should reside in the home (faeries are known to not get along with officials from the church).
- If you're lazy, the faeries might get annoyed with you.
- NEVER insult them, lest they turn on you.
- Don't try to catch them in the act of growing plants in the garden, etc.
- Don't give your typical household elves like brownies any clothing gifts…they will leave.
- Don't thank them for their help or presence.

Faeries are fussy about where they live and visit. They can often be found in the untamed, unspoiled places in nature. If you have a gardener or landscaping service, take over the lawn duty yourself. Garden faeries don't like to be disturbed by people other than the ones they know. Add a small fountain or waterfall to your garden if budget allows. If you happen to have a stump of an old tree, designate this as the faeries' sacred space. Or arrange a circle of stones. Circles are a favorite hang-out spot for faeries. Create faery houses out of bird houses and other natural materials and place them in a safe spot in the garden. This is where you can leave offerings, as well. Make sure no one disturbs this area.

Wrapping It Up

I hope in writing The Otherworldly Household, I have inspired you and guided you in transforming your home from plain and mundane to Otherworldly. I have said it once and I'll say it until the witchy lady sings – make your home magical in your own way. You do not have to carbon copy every suggestion I've given here. Take what you feel resonates and leave behind the rest. I believe you'll find as time goes on and you put a little effort into each room, your home will transform and become a place where you feel loved, protected, and in touch with the Spirit World.

References

Lecouteux, C. (2013). *The Tradition of Household Spirits: Ancestral Lore and Practices*. Inner Traditions.

McCoy, E. (2002). *A Witch's Guide to Faery Folk: How to Work With the Elemental World*. LLewellyn's Publications.

Printed in Great Britain
by Amazon